Also by Luiz Alfredo Garcia-Roza

The Silence of the Rain
December Heat
Southwesterly Wind

A Window in
Copacabana

A NOVEL

A Window in
Copacabana

Luiz Alfredo
GARCIA-ROZA

Translated by Benjamin Moser

Henry Holt and Company
New York

Henry Holt and Company, LLC
Publishers since 1866
115 West 18th Street
New York, New York 10011

Henry Holt® is a registered trademark of
Henry Holt and Company, LLC.

Originally published in Brazil in 2001 under the title *Uma Janela em Copacabana*
by Companhia das Letras, Sao Paulo

Library of Congress Cataloging-in-Publication Data
Garcia-Roza, L. A. (Luiz Alfredo)
[Janela em Copacabana. English]
A window in Copacabana : an Inspector Espinosa mystery / Luiz Alfredo
Garcia-Roza ; translated by Benjamin Moser.—1st American ed.
    p.   cm.
ISBN-13: 978-0-8050-7438
ISBN-10: 0-8050-7438-4
I. Title.
PQ9698.17.A745J3613   2005
869.3'42—dc22   2004052336

First American Edition 2005

Printed in the United States of America
1   3   5   7   9   10   8   6   4   2

A Window in
Copacabana

PART 1

1

At the end of the afternoon, the big digital clock on the corner announced that it was one hundred degrees. Day or night, it was all the same, and inside the car it was invariably sweltering. For hours, they'd been inhaling a nauseating mixture of odors: sweat, half-eaten sandwiches, and bus exhaust. It didn't matter whether they drove faster or slowed down; in the middle of rush hour, the air entering through the window didn't camouflage the stench or take the edge off the heat. The wet burden of sweat clung to the body like the cold skin of a reptile. They were almost happy when the call came from an address only a few blocks away.

The building was old and the hallway leading to the elevators had seen its original shops divided into little stalls, where unkempt entrepreneurs sold bric-a-brac and offered their services as plumbers, gas repairmen, electricians, manicurists, tailors, or card readers. Even though the building was located on a busy section of the Avenida Copacabana, the stalls inside were almost exclusively patronized by the residents of the more than one hundred apartments in the building itself. Only two of the four elevators worked, and the floor-indicator lights were broken or turned off on both.

They exited on the tenth floor and went down one flight

of stairs. They didn't want to be surprised. They didn't know exactly what they were protecting themselves against, but they'd learned to be careful. The man in front moved slowly down the dark hallway, eyes focused on the strip of light emerging from the door to apartment 910. One of his hands aimed his gun at the ceiling and the other felt the way along the wall. A voice emerged from the half-opened door, but the breathing of his colleague just behind him obscured the words. The call had mentioned murder with a firearm. He thought about how well those words applied to his everyday life. Ever since he'd been sent back to regular duty, he'd seen nothing but violence, and murder with a firearm wasn't even the worst of it. In the little training he'd had before hitting the street, they hadn't allowed him to fire more than half a dozen times—to save ammo, they'd said—but the training had included something they called psychological preparation. The girl who taught the classes used the word "psychology" like she used lipstick: to pretty up her mouth. The kid didn't know anything about psychology, but he did understand violence. He'd lived with it since the day he was born. His twenty-two years of life, all spent in the favela, had accustomed him to all kinds of violence, from criminals and drug runners as well as from the police force itself. He'd moved out less than a month before. Cops were being killed; the precinct had, in fact, taken him out of there. Slums were no place for a policeman. There, the law of God was the only law above the drug dealers.

Now he was less than two feet from the door and he

could hear a man's crackly voice, the tone never varying, like a child reciting a lesson to his teacher. He felt the sweat running down his neck: sweat from nerves, not heat. He didn't hear any other voice; maybe the man was talking on the phone. The door was only slightly ajar, and before he stuck his head into the light, he cupped his hand around his ear to listen more closely. Behind his back, he pushed away his partner: the breathing was too loud. He risked a quick glance. He could see only a small corner of the living room. On his first try he made out part of a wall, the end of a small table, and something that looked like an old man in a wheelchair. He waited a few seconds and looked again. The old man was still talking. It was indeed a wheelchair, and he wasn't talking on the phone but with someone sitting in front of him, outside the policeman's field of vision. He made a sign to his partner and pushed open the door, hoping that it wouldn't make a sound. The few inches yielded a wider opening into the room. Now he had an unobstructed view of the old man and the wheelchair, but he still couldn't see his audience. He knocked softly on the door with his knuckle. The old man didn't move or change his tone of voice; he just kept talking. The old man was, in fact, talking to someone seated on the sofa. The other man's shirt was stained red.

The first thing that caught Espinosa's eye was the slit in her skirt, which revealed part of her thigh as she walked. Seated next to the door, he had an ample view of the street, and even before she walked in front of the bar, it was the hint of leg flashing beneath her skirt with each supple movement that distinguished her from the other women passing by. She was about thirty-five. She had a good body, nice legs, and a face whose attractiveness was diminished by a fatigued expression and unkempt hair. The detail of her skirt made her look bold rather than vulgar. He watched the movement of her legs, now revealing, now hiding her thighs, until she passed the café and exited his field of vision.

Espinosa turned his attention back to the cappuccino he'd started to drink and concentrated on the foam covered with cinnamon powder. A few sips later, he was still thinking about the woman when she entered the café. He hadn't expected her to come back. He saw her walk up to the cash register and then look for a seat on the balcony. He decided her return on this hot summer afternoon was a gift from the gods, and he felt within his rights to examine her more closely. What he'd seen when she'd walked by was confirmed by a more detailed inspection. She had perfect legs and a pretty face, with small age lines around her mouth and eyes. These added a note of experience to the youthfulness of her body. She really did look tired, and her hair needed attention, though her hands and skin were well tended. She wasn't paying attention to anything or anyone, simply staring at her coffee cup. Not out of modesty. Someone who walks through a crowded downtown wearing a tight skirt slit up the side isn't exactly concerned about modesty. He soon realized that she wasn't attracting as much attention as she had at the beginning. Not all the men were looking at her; in fact, besides him, only one teenage waiter with bad acne was looking at the woman who stood in front of the bar, back turned, hiding her half-opened skirt.

His thoughts wandered to the possible reasons for her tired (or was it sad?) face; it took him a while to realize that the buzzing coming from his coat pocket was his phone. Just as he answered, the woman also took a cell phone out of her purse. Both spoke at the same time. Unfortunately, he thought, not with each other. As she spoke, her eyes drifted past Espinosa without seeing him, while he looked at her and tried to concentrate on what his assistant, Detective Welber, was telling him.

"Officer, another colleague has been killed."

"Who?"

"Silveira, from the Third Precinct."

"I don't know him."

"He'd been around, but not many people knew him."

7

"Where are you?"

"At the scene. Praça do Lido, on the side facing the beach."

"He was killed on the street?"

"Sort of. The square is fenced off. He was found seated on one of the benches."

"I'm on my way."

When he hung up, she was gone. He hadn't talked to Welber for more than a few seconds; she couldn't have disappeared. He walked to the door and looked around. The pedestrian traffic was intense, and she could have gone in any one of four different directions. He didn't know what he would do if he saw her walking away. He wasn't a Don Juan—never had been. He thought that getting married had forced him to lose sight of the rituals of courtship. Ten years of marriage had produced a kind of emotional myopia. Ever since he and his wife had split up, he'd been trying to retool his approach, to learn new ways of doing things, to move into new territories. But he'd only managed to convince himself of one thing: focusing for too long on one object hadn't improved his vision; it had simply made him nearsighted, as well as a mediocre husband and an inadequate father. He'd devoted the last decade to trying to recoup the lost time.

He walked to the subway, thinking that it would be quite a coincidence to run into her waiting for the same train to Copacabana. At three-thirty the platform of Cinelândia station was fairly empty, though even if it hadn't been he thought he would have been able to pick her out of a crowd. But she wasn't there.

He'd taken the afternoon off to buy a new electric toaster and browse in the secondhand bookstores downtown. He didn't like malls; he liked downtown, with its foot traffic and diverse architecture. He'd barely gotten started when the phone call came through. He was aware that he was not being perfectly honest about needing to come downtown for a toaster or a used-book store; both were available closer to home. And neither justified the absence of the chief of the Twelfth Precinct, on a Monday afternoon, from his workplace in Copacabana: but these trivial errands let him dream of a life outside the police. Every once in a while the desire for a change of pace suddenly surged within him. The spark could be a story in a paper reporting that cops controlled prostitution in several different parts of the city, or a weekend spent exclusively with Irene. The situations elicited entirely different responses—dismay in the first case, attraction in the second—each signaling the silent and almost imperceptible process of distancing himself from something. He wasn't sure what, but it had started a while ago and it worried him intensely. Until he actually made up his mind, a walk through downtown Rio was an effective remedy, though he knew that it was only a placebo.

On his way to the Praça do Lido, he thought about books. It wasn't really the books themselves he liked—he wasn't a bibliophile, and his books didn't even have proper shelves. They were just piled up next to the living room wall, one row arranged vertically, another horizontally, and so on, until they rose taller than Espinosa himself. It was narratives he sought in books, well-told stories. His maternal grandmother, who had educated him, had instilled in him a love of reading. In any case, that afternoon, downtown, he hadn't bought a single book, or a toaster; he was simply distracted by a woman's leg. He was sorry about missing the bookstores, but he was secretly satisfied about the toaster. His toaster had had the same problem for almost a year: it toasted only one side of the bread. He'd grown used to the ritual of toasting one side of the bread, then flipping it around and waiting for the other side to be ready. Before he'd even gotten rid of the toaster, he'd already missed it.

He got to the Praça do Lido a little before four in the afternoon. Located in the first third of Copacabana Beach, the plaza took up half a block; the other was occupied by a public school. The school was on the side facing the Avenida Copacabana, while the square faced the Avenida Atlântica, in front of the ocean. At that hour, it would have been occupied by children and senior citizens, if the yellow police tape hadn't kept them back. Covered with a piece of black plastic that Espinosa identified as a reconfigured garbage bag, the body sat on the bench, in the same position in which it had been discovered by the companion of an elderly woman who often visited the square.

As soon as he bent under the yellow tape, Espinosa spotted his assistant walking toward him. Welber had lost the freshman jauntiness he'd had when Espinosa first met him. But he still had the same enthusiasm that two years earlier had led him to take a bullet directed at his chief. Not out of heroism—though he was capable of it—but because he was younger and quicker.

"What happened?" the officer asked.

"Silveira from the Third Precinct . . . He was shot in the neck while sitting on the bench in the garden. Nobody saw or heard anything. He was discovered by the nurse, who was with an old lady in a wheelchair who comes every afternoon to the square. She sat on one end of the bench with the wheelchair next to her, talking to the lady. . . . According to her, it wasn't exactly a conversation, since she was the only one talking. Half an hour later, she noticed that the man seated at the other end of the bench, whose head was resting on his chest, hadn't moved an inch. At first she thought he was asleep, but then she noticed something was wrong. She spoke to him, but he didn't answer. She tried again, but the man didn't budge. She got up to look, and that's when she saw the blood on his collar. She got one of the maintenance men and asked him to call the police. It was around three in the afternoon."

"Where is the woman?"

"On that bench over there. She says she can't stay; she has to take the old lady home."

"And what about her? Did she see or hear anything?"

"She can't talk. The nurse says she can understand the

occasional grunt, but she doesn't think the old lady knows what's going on around her. In any case, she didn't seem to be scared or shocked by anything."

"Why didn't they sit on an empty bench?"

"All the others were taken."

"No witnesses?"

"None. Nobody saw anything unusual."

"What did you find out?"

"Not much. He was shot point-blank while sitting on the bench, his back to the grassy part of the park. The murderer could have come up from behind, across the grass, silently, with the weapon hidden behind a newspaper or inside a bag. The noise of the traffic from the two avenues is enough to muffle the noise of a gun with a silencer. A professional job."

"What was a detective from the Third Precinct, downtown, doing at three in the afternoon on a weekday sitting on a park bench in Copacabana?"

Espinosa had hardly finished the question when he realized that it could apply to himself as well. What had he been doing at that same hour, sitting in a café downtown? If he'd been shot in the head, what would his death have to do with the fact that he had been drinking a cappuccino downtown? No investigator, no matter how expert, could have guessed that he was there only because he'd randomly decided to sit in that café at that moment, his eye attracted by a slit skirt.

"Try to find out if he lives around here, or if some relative does. The park must have someone in charge of it; talk to him, ask if he'd ever seen Detective Silveira. I'll go talk to the chief of the Third Precinct. Did anyone go through his pockets?"

"I did. Wallet, ID card, cell phone, keys, notepad, pen, handkerchief. His weapon's in his belt. Nothing written on the notepad."

"Could anyone have done it before you?"

"The cops who answered the call, but if anyone went through his pockets they don't seem to have taken anything. His wallet still has his credit cards, checks, and some money."

"If you've already taken down the names and addresses of the woman and the nurse, you can let them go. If Silveira met people at this park, the caretaker must have noticed something. Squeeze him a little. I'll see you back at the station."

The station was five blocks down the Avenida Atlântica and two to the right, up Hilário de Gouveia. Whenever possible, Espinosa preferred to take the Avenida Atlântica. The soft breeze kept the sea calm, with small waves, and seagulls flew in groups toward the Cagarras Islands. Why would someone choose a public place, a park, to murder a policeman? One answer: because no one would think to do it there. Another possibility: because he happened to be there. Third possibility: because the cop and the murderer had arranged to meet there. There were other options, but since the walk to the station wasn't very long, Espinosa contented himself with those three. The third was probably the most likely. Now, if the cop had arranged to meet the murderer there, and was waiting for him while peacefully sitting on a bench, it was because the cop didn't know that he was a murderer, or because he knew but it didn't occur to him that he himself would be the victim. It probably wasn't a meeting arranged to settle scores, or the cop would have been more careful. The laid-back way he'd waited for the other's arrival suggested that they knew each other. They might even have been friends. Espinosa eliminated the idea that they were meeting to exchange some merchandise. The location was too visible, and there was only one exit. The breeze from the sea took the edge off the heat and even made the walk fairly pleasant, provided, of course, that Espinosa stayed in the shade.

As soon as he arrived at the station, he called the Third Precinct. The officer who answered was new at his post, and sounded young. As they didn't know each other, Espinosa kept things formal.

"Sir, I'm sorry about what happened to your detective. I've just come from the scene, and I'd like to discuss a couple of matters regarding the victim."

"Thank you, Officer Espinosa. I've only been at the Third for a little more than a month, and I don't know all the officers here yet. I had little contact with Detective Silveira. I only knew that he'd been around for a long time, and that he was biding his time till retirement."

"Did he work or was he working on any case that could have left him open to a revenge killing?"

"Not as far as I know."

"Any declared enemies?"

"I don't think so. He was a nice guy; he had good relationships with his colleagues."

"Well, in any case, thank you. Don't hesitate to call me if there's anything you need."

"Thanks a lot."

Welber arrived forty minutes later.

"Nobody knows anything, nobody saw anything, and the guy in charge of the park had never seen Silveira. You'd think he died of a heart attack and not a shot in the head. Some people even said he might have been a victim of a stray bullet."

"Maybe, but it strayed right into his head."

"Did you talk to the Third Precinct?"

"I did. According to them, Silveira was an exemplary cop, friendly with all his colleagues. In my opinion, if he was so exemplary and beloved, he's not being mourned very loudly. Up until now, nobody's bothered to ask what happened."

"And what do you think happened?"

"We could be dealing with two connected crimes: today's and Ramos's murder last week. They have some things in common. First, obviously, both victims were cops. Second, the way the murderer shot them: one fatal shot, no struggle, no confusion. Third, they were both killed in front of other people, which made no difference at all: Ramos was killed in front of his father, who has Alzheimer's and can't understand what is happening around him; Silveira was killed in plain view, but nobody saw anything. Same style, same murderer. It's a good bet."

3

It was a ten-minute walk from the station to his house. When he took the longer route, down the Avenida Copacabana, passing through the Galeria Menescal to pick up a snack, it took a few more minutes. He had the choice of three different cuisines, but his gastronomic options still felt limited: the Arabic place in the Galeria Menescal, the German takeout in the little frozen-foods store near his house, or the Italian, represented in his freezer by some spaghetti and lasagna. That afternoon, because he'd chosen the shorter route, it was going to have to be the spaghetti. He didn't complain. When he wanted to eat well, he went to a restaurant.

It was already after seven, it was still light out, and there were plenty of pedestrians on the street. He hadn't walked more than two blocks before he felt a hand on his shoulder and heard his name. It took him a few seconds to recognize the face and remember the name of the detective, who had just been transferred to his precinct.

"Nestor."

"I'm sorry if I surprised you, sir."

"Is something the matter?"

"I'm sorry to come after you on the street."

"No problem. What's going on?"

"Nothing, Officer. I mean, these murders, two colleagues, Ramos and Silveira . . ."

". . . and you're scared."

"It's not that I'm scared. I haven't done anything to make anyone want to kill me."

"Did the two who died do anything?"

"I don't know, sir, but they must have, or it wouldn't have happened."

"No need for us to stand here in the middle of the sidewalk. Walk me two blocks and tell me what's worrying you."

"It's not that I'm worried, Officer, but there's a rumor going around that we haven't seen the end of it. . . . Two guys have already died, and I think more people are going to get killed."

"Who says more people are going to get killed?"

"Nobody in particular, just rumors—people are saying it on the phone."

"So you mean someone's trying to spread the rumor, and it seems to be working."

They paused in front of a newspaper kiosk, and as he scanned the magazine covers, Espinosa tried to figure out why Nestor had approached him. The detective seemed to be reciting a text he'd already rehearsed. It wasn't so much what he was saying but the fact that he'd approached Espinosa on the street; that was significant. Espinosa knew almost nothing about the detective, just what was recorded in his file. The man seemed to feel personally endangered, even though he was trying to act nonchalant. He wasn't a very good actor. If he was, in fact, feeling threatened, he must know why the other two had died, but he obviously wasn't going to blurt it out here and now. Espinosa paid for the two magazines he'd selected and resumed walking.

"Why do you think the two murders are connected?"

"I don't think it, sir; I'm absolutely sure of it."

"Why are you so sure?"

"Officer, I've been on the force for almost twenty years. I know a hit when I see one."

"What do you know about the two cops who died?"

"Almost nothing. I knew one of them by sight; we'd spoken on the phone once. The other one I'd seen around a couple of times when I was working on robberies."

"Did you make friends with either of them?"

"Ramos and I worked at the same station for a while. We were colleagues, but I wouldn't call him a friend."

"Did you ever see him afterward?"

"No. After I was transferred I ran into him occasionally."

"Right. So you think they're going to kill more cops?"

"It's what they're saying. We have to find out who the nut is who's doing this."

"Do you think the guy's a nut?"

"He's got to be. Someone who goes around killing cops has got to be crazy."

"I'm not sure. . . . I think the murderer is too efficient and careful to be crazy."

"But you agree that we've got to find the guy as soon as possible?"

"Of course. At least before my number comes up."

"Sir . . ."

"Just kidding. I don't think two murders is enough to draw any conclusions. It could just be a coincidence."

"Officer, I just want to say that I'm there for anything you need. . . . After all, they were our colleagues."

"Thanks, I know I can count on you."

"Good night, Chief."

"Good night, Nestor."

Espinosa was struck by how quickly day turned into night in the Rio de Janeiro summer. There was no transition; the director of the scene suddenly dropped the curtain. The phenomenon of dusk was so short-lived that it could be observed only at precisely the right time, on precisely the right beach. And the walk from the station to the Peixoto District wasn't exactly the right beach. By the time he reached Peixoto, it had started getting dark. He crossed the square in the direction of his building.

Despite its name, the Peixoto District wasn't really a separate neighborhood but a rectangle, four hundred meters by two hundred, formed by two main streets and two small cross streets, with a square in the middle. As in a medieval city, the buildings formed a kind of protective wall separating it from the rest of Copacabana. Most of the buildings were only three or four stories high and dated from a time when there was no need for elevators or garages, only a certain taste for French windows opening onto little balconies. Espinosa's apartment was on the third floor of one of these buildings, facing the square.

He opened the living room blinds to let some air in, stuck the frozen pasta in the microwave, sat down on the sofa, looked out at the square, and awaited the three beeps signaling that his dinner was ready.

An hour after he finished eating, he was still thinking about Nestor. What had he really been trying to say? Espinosa barely knew him, and the little that he'd seen in Nestor's dossier was neither to his credit nor to his detriment.

He dedicated the following two hours to examining a book that, along with a few hundred others, he'd inherited from his grandmother. Every once in a while his grandmother had felt the need to purge some of the thousands of books piled in two rooms of her apartment, and these were destined for the apartment of her grandson, who had also inherited her habit of stockpiling books. Their styles were different: hers were anarchic piles, his orderly stacks against the wall. They shared a disdain for shelving.

He'd liked the book's title, *Phantom Lady*, and admired its perfect condition, miraculously conserved since 1942. His knowledge of English was passable, better for reading than for conversation. He hadn't recognized the author's name, William Irish, until he'd learned somewhere else that William Irish was the pseudonym of Cornell Woolrich. He liked the title of the first chapter, "The Hundred and Fiftieth Day Before the Execution." An author who began a book announcing that someone would be murdered within a hundred and fifty days, and whose following chapters built up to "A Day After the Execution," was worth reading.

The next morning, the rumor about the cop murderer had flown around the station, and was now a source of concern for Inspector Ramiro, chief of the detectives in the Twelfth Precinct.

"Two murders don't make a series," Espinosa repeated to Ramiro.

"I know, sir, but the guys are worried."

"There's not even necessarily a connection."

"Sir, you know as well as I do that these murders are connected, and that more are on the way."

"Yesterday Nestor sought me out on the street. He thinks the same thing."

"Which Nestor, the one from this precinct?"

"That's right. He wanted to know what I thought about it, and he accosted me as I was walking home."

"Why didn't he talk to you here at the station?"

"Probably because he didn't want people to know he was concerned."

"Approaching you on the street shows that he is."

"He offered his help in the investigation."

"Everyone wants to help."

"They must think it will protect them."

After the inspector left, Espinosa got out his notes on the

two murders and listened to what he'd recorded on his little Dictaphone. Not much. In fact, almost nothing. At the
scene of the first murder, no one could describe the person
who'd come into the building pushing the wheelchair. A
few witnesses had said the person was a female nurse; others, a male nurse. The witnesses said that they'd noticed
the old man and the wheelchair but not the person accom-
panying them. Besides, they'd all agreed, the landlord
never fixed the light bulbs in the hall.

"We live in the dark—it's surprising more people don't
get murdered—but I'm sure the person with them was a
man," the lady who'd ridden the elevator with the wheelchair declared.

"How can you be so sure?"

"Because of his height. I was squished into the elevator
in order to make room. Three people, besides the wheelchair with the man in it. It was easy to see that the nurse
was a man."

"And can you tell us if he was black or white?"

"Let me think. . . . He was black . . . black and big."

"Besides tall, as you already said."

"Well, maybe he wasn't all that tall," the lady answered.

"And maybe not so black," Espinosa completed.

"Sir, people can get confused with the lights out in the
building."

"But you're sure it wasn't a tall woman?"

"Only if it was a very tall woman."

She hadn't seen the nurse, male or female, leave the

building. The possibility that someone could provide a description of the murderer was extremely remote. The only actual witness to the crime had Alzheimer's. The cops who'd arrived on the scene first had found a card in a clear plastic envelope in the old man's pocket. There was a contact name, address, and phone number. The phone number was the victim's. The old man and the dead cop were father and son. The apartment was used for the policeman's professional meetings, according to the doorman and the management.

Welber had managed to learn that the detective and his father met once a week, always in the apartment. The old man liked to talk, but the stories he told and the people he discussed had no basis in reality. He didn't recognize anyone and couldn't remember names, and apparently he had no idea that the man he saw regularly was his son. He was a widower and lived in a building on the same block as his son. He was taken care of by visiting nurses—women generally—who stayed for twenty-four hours at a time.

Welber also learned that on the afternoon of the murder, two hours before the end of the shift, the woman who'd accompanied the old man had been relieved early. She'd been very grateful for her colleague's generosity.

"Her colleague? Man or woman?" Espinosa asked.

"Right. . . . Well, you know . . ."

"Know what?"

"Not so much of a man . . ."

"Gay?"

"You can usually tell, right?"

"But aren't all the nurses women?"

"No, not at all, there are men and women . . . and lots of homosexuals. Some clients prefer them because they're as strong as men and as gentle as women."

Welber had asked the woman, "What does he look like?"

"He's got blond, shoulder-length hair, a blond mustache, big thick glasses, light eyes, green or blue. . . . Taller than I am, and I think he's got a little beer belly. . . . A little buck-toothed, so he talks a little funny. But a lot of queers tend to talk like that, right?"

"You didn't know that he was going to replace you?"

"We don't always know. I don't think I know half the people who work there. The agency has a lot of turnover."

The nursing service knew no one by that description.

The second crime had been committed even more out in the open than the first, yet no one could provide the slightest detail about the murderer. In both cases, maximum visibility meant maximum blindness. The forensic people hadn't turned up anything at either scene.

The information relating to the second murder shared one detail with the first: both victims were mediocre policemen who hadn't stood out in any way. Their dossiers might as well have been blank, even though they had been on the force for years. They'd transferred precincts often, so they hadn't made many friends on the force. There was another coincidence. Their residential addresses were both in Copacabana: Ramos's was the scene of his murder, and Silveira's was located only a block from the Praça do Lido, where he'd been shot. Yet nothing Welber had learned suggested that the men had actually lived in these apartments. Doormen, management, and neighbors agreed that both were discreet people who never caused any problems and received few visitors, two or three friends at most. Sometimes their girlfriends showed up, but only rarely, though almost all of their meetings included a woman. "Important detail," Welber added in the oral report he gave Espinosa. "No one, at either address, knew that they were cops. They identified themselves as traveling salesmen, which explained why they were rarely home. They kept their private lives as obscure as their professional ones."

"That's pretty efficient," Espinosa remarked to Welber as they left the building to go to lunch.

"Why do you say that?"

"Because nobody can work anywhere for twenty years, even with frequent transfers, without anybody noticing them, unless they're trying to be invisible."

"Why do you think they didn't want to be noticed?"

"I'm not sure yet, but we'll find out."

"After we find somewhere to eat, of course."

"Right."

"As long as it's not McDonald's."

"Of course."

"Seated, not standing."

"Fine."

"My girlfriend says I can't keep eating in a hurry, standing at a counter, and that fast food is fattening and has a lot of cholesterol."

"She's right. She's taking good care of you. Soon she'll be taking care of you full-time."

It wasn't easy for Welber to find Ramos's mistress. Maria Rita hadn't attended the funeral or the wake; the woman who mourned him was his wife, of whose existence nobody had been aware. From the police, only the official representatives, including Espinosa and Welber, were present. Maria Rita was discovered days later via Ramos's phone bill, which included regular calls to her number.

The same story emerged a week later, when they located Silveira's mistress, Aparecida. The similarity in the details was striking: same kind of apartment, same kind of lover, same secretive lifestyle. Ramos and Silveira had led twin lives, and had shared twin deaths.

4

In three days, there had been no murders in the precinct, only a frustrated bank robbery, two attempted hotel burglaries (one assailant wounded), and a few dozen petty crimes, several of which included tourists. No progress had been made on the investigation of the murdered policemen.

It was already after seven on Friday night when Espinosa decided to head home. He selected the shortest route; he wasn't interested in doing anything on the way. A misty rain was falling, which made people walk faster or hover beneath awnings. He planned to take a bath and have dinner somewhere pleasant; he didn't feel like warming something up and doing the dishes. The streetlights were already on; Espinosa attributed the feeling that he was being followed to recent events, and to the eerie twilight. He remembered how Nestor had approached him at almost precisely the same place. He walked a little farther and stopped at the same kiosk where he had paused with the detective; he looked around, examined the magazines for a while in order to see if any of the other pedestrians lingered, but nobody struck him as suspicious. He continued on his way.

The choice of a restaurant in Rio de Janeiro in summertime is influenced as much by the quality of the food as by the quality of the air-conditioning. The small Italian place where he had lunch on Saturdays satisfied on both counts, and the owner was always friendly. He'd long since grown used to eating alone. Instead of talking, he observed the people around him, without attracting their attention. He'd choose someone at one of the neighboring tables and speculate on what their life had been like, gauging their clothing, the way they spoke, or the person they were with. It was a good exercise, but it didn't lead to any absolute knowledge, since he had no way to follow up. Without any objective criteria, however, he knew when he was close and when he was stumped. Depending on the occasion, he sometimes invented fantastically detailed biographies. Sometimes he practiced on himself. Occasionally he spun these stories out so far that he lost any connection with the original person, and they lost their identity completely.

When he left the restaurant, the rain had stopped and the sidewalk was dry. The best route home was a few blocks down the Avenida Atlântica and then a perpendicular approach to the Peixoto District. He hadn't been walking ten minutes when he was once again struck by the feeling that he was being followed. Since it had been raining, there were fewer people out, which made it easier to isolate a possible stalker. He walked a little farther, looking for a dry bench. He sat down and studied the stream of people who followed, checking to see if any of them slowed down. Just like the first time, he found no candidates. He waited a few minutes, got up, and went home.

He considered Saturday mornings special, as opposed to Sundays, which, as far as he was concerned, had no reason for existing. While he read two newspapers—instead of the one he looked at on weekdays—he drank two cups of coffee and allowed himself a double helping of toast, which he smeared with excess jam. The main thing he did on Saturday mornings was concoct extremely detailed and ambitious plans for his life or his home, none of which were fated to leave the drawing board.

When he and his wife had split up, she'd taken the furniture and all the domestic utensils. He himself had insisted on it. Since she was taking their son, it didn't make sense to divide things up. Except in Solomonic parables, it didn't make sense to divvy up a kid. He'd kept the apartment where he'd lived since childhood—first with his parents, then with his grandmother, who'd taken care of him until he was grown, and, eventually, with his wife and son. His parents had been killed in an automobile accident when he was fourteen, and his only living relative was his maternal grandmother. She had stayed with him until he was nineteen, at which point she'd returned to her own apartment, which she hadn't been able to rent out during the intervening years because of the enormous quantities of books, which threatened to devour any tenant. From her, Espinosa had inherited his taste for reading. Neither of them were intellectuals. They simply liked books. She, because she was a translator; he, because he liked good stories. In the careful mess that now reigned in his apartment, great literary classics shared space with the old Coleção

Amarela crime novels he'd inherited from his father. The current austere look of his apartment was not an aesthetic choice but the result of a decision to keep only the bare minimum of things required for the function and comfort of the place's only inhabitant. Shelving was thus unnecessary, even for someone with more than a thousand books piled up against the living room wall.

The Saturday morning sky was serenely blue, and the heat was not unpleasant. Whenever he could, he preferred not to use the air conditioner. Not to save money, although that was occasionally necessary, but because the machine dried out the air and set up an artificial barrier between him and the outside world. Air-conditioning placed a city in parentheses: it might as well be Paris or New York as Rio de Janeiro. Air conditioners all had the same temperature, the same smell, and the same opaque noise that neutralized any local sounds. He pushed his rocking chair over to the French window, facing the mini-balcony, and rested his feet on the cast-iron rail. He was finishing up the first newspaper when the telephone rang. Normally he'd let the answering machine get it, but on Saturday morning it was always possible that it might be a pleasant call.

"Sir, I apologize for calling at this hour—"

"No problem."

"—but they got Nestor."

"What do you mean?"

"They killed him. Like the other two."

30

Nestor was found dead in a small apartment on the Rua Ministro Viveiros de Castro, near the Avenida Prado Júnior, at the far edge of Copacabana. When Espinosa arrived at the apartment, Freire, the researcher from the Criminological Institute and an acquaintance, was talking to Welber.

"Freire, Welber. . . . Anything?"

"Just like the other one," the researcher answered.

"What's like the other one?" Espinosa asked.

"A shot in the neck, gun fired from a few inches away."

Freire rarely spoke, and when he did his delivery was staccato. Welber, seeing that Freire had run out of things to say that day, added the details he'd managed to piece together.

"Nestor was seated with his back toward the door, watching TV and drinking beer. He was already on his second bottle. There were two cups on the coffee table, but only one had been used. The phone rang, he picked it up, and was talking when he was hit in the neck. The phone fell and dangled next to his arm. The money in his wallet, his ID, and his weapon are all on the bedside table. Apparently nothing was stolen. He also had a cell phone on the table; we checked the last call dialed and got the apartment phone number. The murderer must have been standing outside the apartment door, talking to Nestor on the cell phone. With Nestor distracted by the noise of the television and the phone call, the murderer came in and shot him."

"We definitely have a pattern: a cop, a single point-blank shot, no witnesses," answered Espinosa.

Like the other two victims, Nestor had been practically a

stranger to his colleagues. Little or nothing was known about his private life, and his service record was barely enough to fill half a page. One glance was enough to take in the whole apartment.

This was clearly not someone's home. The only businesses in the area were a few bars and sleazy hangouts, and most of the apartments were studios. Surveillance of comings and goings in the area was nonexistent. Nestor's apartment had the advantage of looking out onto the street. The view was not one of the city's more spectacular, but it made the interior feel a little less cramped. The kitchenette, which was barely larger than a wardrobe, contained a small refrigerator with a bottle of water and a few beers. There was no food and only one jar of coffee crystals and one bottle of liquid sweetener; in the single closet were some sheets, two towels, and a change of clothes hanging from a solitary wire hanger; nothing in the bathroom indicated that anyone lived there. The apartment was as impersonal as a hotel room.

"It seems like a meeting place," Espinosa said after looking around and opening a few drawers. "His weapon wasn't close at hand; to get it, he'd have had to get past the bed. Not where he would have left it if he'd been expecting a dangerous visitor. Like the other two, he was expecting a friend or acquaintance."

"There's only one more item on the checklist," Espinosa said to Welber.

"What's that?"

"Find the mistress."

Freire was packing up his working materials.

"There are no fingerprints on the phone or on the door-knob. The lock wasn't forced. When the forensic people get the bullet, I'll be able to tell you if it's from the same weapon as the other two. As soon as I've got something, I'll let you know."

"What do you think?" Welber asked as soon as Freire left.

"One member of the club is bumping off the rest of the team."

Both of them were looking at the cadaver when the cell phone rang. Espinosa answered.

"Hello!" a young voice said. "Cíntia?"

5

The interview didn't last fifteen minutes, and if it had been up to Espinosa it wouldn't have lasted fifteen seconds. But the secretary of security had recommended that officers make themselves available to the press to showcase the government's efforts to wipe out police corruption.

"Sergeant, were the murdered cops part of the so-called bad apples?"

"Was this one bad apple killing others?"

"Do you think we're seeing an attempt to destroy evidence?"

"Do you think the police department has finally found a way to clean itself up?"

Espinosa had a sense of humor, but he didn't appreciate irony. As far as he was concerned, the sooner the interview ended, the better. Besides, it was hard to be friendly on a Monday morning. He agreed to let himself be filmed at the entrance to the station, in front of the arch with the words "Twelfth Precinct" on the facade. After a few minutes, Welber rescued his boss and sent away the reporters.

"You did well, sir. . . . They were trying to provoke you, but you stayed calm. I was afraid they'd tick you off."

"Do you have an aspirin?"

Espinosa answered a few more phone calls from reporters wanting to know if there was a serial killer murdering policemen or if the force was cleaning house. Then he went to lunch. Not because he was hungry, but because he didn't want to answer any more calls.

He headed toward the beach, thinking back to the afternoon when Nestor had approached him. He remembered noting more curiosity than fear in the detective.

He left McDonald's holding a bag with a burger, a milk shake, and fries. Welber's girlfriend would have disapproved. He sat down on a sidewalk bench on the Avenida Atlântica and got ready for a lunch with a sea view. In fact, he neither ate lunch nor looked at the sea: this wasn't a proper lunch and he wasn't paying attention to the view, though he seemed to be staring right at it. He tried to remember Nestor's words: "I haven't done anything to make anyone want to kill me." He'd seemed quite certain that more people would die. What the detective didn't seem to suspect was that he'd be the next victim. "I haven't done anything to make anyone want to kill me" was ambiguous: it implied that he'd done something, but nothing that deserved the death penalty.

The problem with eating lunch on a public bench was that you were invariably forced to share your space. A boy who must have been about six years old but didn't look older than three or four stared at Espinosa before leaving with the fries. "I haven't done anything to make anyone want to kill me." That's where you were wrong, son. You had indeed; you just didn't know what. The boy came back with another kid as small as he was, who left with the Big Mac. "More people are going to get killed," Nestor had also said. What Espinosa wanted to know, seeing the two boys walk off, was who, and when.

He sat looking at the ocean, finishing his milk shake. The shade of the almond tree was pleasant, and the view was included in the price of the lunch. His reverie was interrupted by someone sitting down on the bench. It was Welber.

"Sir, I thought you'd be out here somewhere."

"Welber, if you'd gotten here a couple of minutes ago you could have eaten with us."

Welber didn't understand the reference and didn't try. He knew his boss.

"I didn't come here to eat with you," he said.

"What's going on?"

"Besides the three murders, nothing. For now."

"If there's one more murder, every cop in town is going to be walking around with an itchy trigger finger."

"More or less."

"What are we going to do to avoid that?"

"Get the murderer."

"The problem isn't the murderer," Espinosa said.

"No?"

"I think he's been hired to do the job. He's just a tool, not the real cause of the deaths. Or, if you like, he's the immediate cause but not the ultimate cause. He could be replaced by someone else."

"Why are you saying that?"

"Because the three murders were too clean. Someone who's killing for hate or revenge riddles the body with bul-

lets and spits on top of it. These murders were clean, silent,
surgical; there was no passion, revenge, emotion: cold as
ice. Whoever killed them was hired by someone. And fur-
thermore, the real criminal is trying to send a message to
other potential victims, a message that only they can understand. The ones who didn't get the memo, including
Nestor, died. There's a pattern to the killings and there's a
pattern to the victims. They're all cops who never stood
out, who lived hidden lives, and who were as invisible and
silent as their deaths."

"A lot of people seem to think the message is meant for
them."

"Then they have some idea of the motive."

"What are we going to do to stop the rumors?"

"We're going to examine the lives of all the dead men
and try to get anything we can from the crime scenes. Of
course it will take more than just one investigator. We've
got to set up a team. I'll leave the technical aspects to
Freire."

The two sat looking at the sea in silence until they rose
to return to the station.

"Who did you eat with, sir?"

"No one you know."

Espinosa settled on three cops. Ramiro, the inspector:
twenty years on the job, head of the detectives, a link between the chief and the rank and file, skilled at interroga-
tion, and an able investigator. It would be a mistake not to

include him. The second choice was Artur, a detective who'd just gotten out of the police academy, intelligent and still untainted by corruption. The third was Welber, his assistant and colleague of several years, whom Espinosa trusted completely. The operational aspects would fall under the purview of Inspector Ramiro.

The first meeting was held behind closed doors on Thursday afternoon. The chief laid out the plan of action.

"We don't know why they're killing cops. If the murderer is killing at random, any one of us could be next, and if he thinks that our investigation could disrupt his plans, he could turn against us. I want to know every step you take. I want a daily report of all your activities. Orally— don't write anything down. Don't use your computer to store data or for e-mail. If you need to interview, remember that you can be followed. You are absolutely prohibited to make any comment, no matter how insignificant, to anyone besides the people in this room. That includes your father, mother, colleague, friend, wife, girlfriend, priest, pastor, or rabbi: when you pray, do it silently and without moving your lips. If you need to make notes during your investigation, destroy anything you don't absolutely need; hide the important stuff where it won't be found. Keep this in mind: from now on, your lives depend on following these rules. This isn't going to be a team investigation. Forget about the normal procedures. At a certain point you're going to investigate your own colleagues. It won't be fun. If anything happens to me, the group is disbanded."

"What do you mean, if anything happens to you?" Artur asked.

"I don't feel endangered, but they may decide to shut down the investigation. Discretion is our best protection. If they know what we're up to, they'll be able to anticipate our next move. You will be more exposed than I am."

"When do we start?"

"Tomorrow. First of all, I want you to find out everything possible about the victims: property, real estate, family, wives, mistresses, friends, trips, hobbies, gambling, debts, health . . . everything."

"Are the meetings always going to be held here?"

"Your individual reports can be given here, but we'll hold our meetings at different places outside the station."

The three were getting up to leave when Espinosa made a final suggestion.

"Whenever possible, I want Artur to work with Ramiro or Welber, at least for a while. One more thing: your colleagues, here and in other precincts, are going to find out about this investigation. In other words, they'll know you're investigating *them*."

It was after seven-thirty by the time he got home. While he was getting undressed, he listened to the messages on his answering machine. There were days when he felt more intensely than others that his skin had been used, over the course of the day, as a trap for every pollutant in the atmosphere, and it was nice to send the day's residue down the shower drain. He was still wrapped in his towel when he returned Irene's call. Her machine picked up.

He'd met Irene during a murder investigation. She and the victim had been close. Once the investigation was over, he and Irene became friends, and as time went by they became a little more than that. She was a graphic designer, financially independent, and lived alone in a pleasant apartment in Ipanema, two blocks from the beach. They often met up, but they never planned their next date. Irene worked in São Paulo as much as in Rio, so they simply saw each other whenever they could. Irene was undemanding, which somehow bothered Espinosa, even though he sincerely preferred to keep things as they were. But he couldn't help thinking that more than a decade of living alone was a sign that something wasn't right. He sometimes wondered whether it would be better either to commit to celibacy consciously or to move in with someone, once and for all. He liked Irene, but he didn't doubt that their relationship had reached a perfect balance, and that any attempt to shift the scales would mean the end.

Irene thought of cops—him in particular—as sleazy. And that was what made Espinosa special for her. Irene balanced her serious professional life with romantic eccentricities. The lesbian relationship she'd had with her murdered friend was one such eccentricity; sleeping with a cop was another.

He took off the towel, put on some shorts, and started pacing around the living room. He didn't feel like listening to music and felt even less like watching TV. He didn't want to eat frozen food, and he didn't want to do the dishes. He made two sandwiches out of black bread and cold cuts, which he took with a bottle of beer to the living room couch. On the coffee table was the book he'd started the week before. He picked it up again, but abandoned it before the end of the chapter. He turned on the TV. Sometimes that worked.

The following hours were marked by a nervousness he rarely experienced. Eventually, the real reason for his anxiety rose to the surface. He was unsure if his resistance to a more stable relationship with Irene had something to do with the homosexual episode in her past. Or episodes: he couldn't be sure there hadn't been others. A few years had passed since then, but certain things are reluctant to leave us, or for us to leave them. Perhaps she still engaged in sporadic relationships of that kind. Or was the relationship with Espinosa the sporadic one? Consciously, he wasn't bothered by Irene's past. Or her present. She was a beautiful woman, deliciously feminine. Her experience with the other woman, or other women, was not a result of too little femininity but of too much of it. That's what she'd told him once, at least. But the fact was that he couldn't get over the prejudices he'd accumulated as a child, in the neighborhood of Fátima, downtown, before he'd come to live in Copacabana. Back then everything was simple: boys were boys, girls were girls, and everyone acted according to the patterns of their sex. There was no confusion. Or at least that's what he'd thought. How much of the boy from Fátima was still alive in him?

6

The early stage of the investigation uncovered several facts, but others remained mysterious. The first was that all three victims had three addresses: one official, one private (which didn't figure on the police registry), and a third where their mistresses lived. The two who died in Copacabana apartments had been killed in their official residences: little apartments used almost exclusively for rendezvous. The unofficial addresses corresponded to upper-middle-class buildings in Barra da Tijuca, where the deceased had lived with their families. Ramiro's job was to visit the widows. He learned that the policemen had spent only three or four nights a week at home; on the other nights, they'd claimed to be working the late shift or performing some other professional duty: following a suspect, working out of town, investigating undercover. Their wives had long since given up on checking out their husbands' excuses; or, because they lived so comfortably, they were no longer interested.

Their mistresses, like the wives, had extremely limited social lives, subsisting even more invisibly than the policemen themselves. None of the murdered men were drug addicts or alcoholics. These facts were gleaned on Friday and over the weekend, and brought to the group's first meeting outside the station house.

The restaurant was not frequented by cops from either of the Copacabana precincts, though that wasn't what had inspired Espinosa to select it. If anyone wanted to know where they were meeting, all they had to do was follow them. The important thing was never to meet in the same place twice. The choice was to be communicated to the others by Espinosa shortly before each meeting.

"I don't care if they see you. I just don't want them to be able to listen in."

The plate of the day was rice with sausage. For Espinosa, anything besides frozen spaghetti was welcome. Welber, attentive to his girlfriend's suggestions, asked for grilled chicken breast; Ramiro and Artur both ordered the special.

Even though all three of them had participated in investigating the addresses and possessions of the dead cops, Ramiro provided the outline, since only he had been in direct contact with the widows.

"It's not for nothing that they hid their real addresses. With a detective's salary, they wouldn't have been able to pay for one of the cars in their garages, much less the houses and apartments they lived in. None of them was married to a rich woman or had won the lottery."

"Family money? Inheritance?"

"Nothing. Them or their wives. But they weren't showoffs. None of the cars were imported or brand-new. One of them lived in a house, the others in apartments; everything was good quality, but nothing spectacular. They didn't give parties or hang out in expensive places."

"The first one you talked to didn't warn the other two that you were coming?"

"No. That's what I find most intriguing. They didn't know about one another; their husbands rarely mentioned their colleagues. Another thing: nobody in the area knew they were cops. It's true that a lot of cops will do anything to deny that they're cops, so as not to draw the attention of drug dealers, but in their case I agree with what the chief said the other day: they seemed to be hiding deliberately. The wives don't know much, and I don't think they're hiding anything. They really seemed not to know. Either they were really out of the loop, or they're really good actresses. I'd bet on the first."

"How did they react to your visit?"

"They thought it was normal for us to investigate their husbands' deaths. They even thanked me for the attention we were giving the case."

"And what about their colleagues in the station, did you have any problems?"

"Not directly," said Ramiro. "But this morning I found this note on top of my desk."

The inspector removed a piece of paper from his pocket, unfolded it, and placed it on the table. It was handwritten, in capital letters: IF YOU LIKE YOUR FAMILY, LEAVE OTHER PEOPLE'S FAMILIES ALONE.

"Any idea who did it?"

"Someone from this precinct, of course. Nobody from outside, even a cop, would risk entering the building, passing by reception, and coming up to the second floor to leave a note on my desk."

"That's the kind of thing I was trying to say last time. It's one thing to fight criminals, another to go after your own colleagues. We're certainly going to have to keep in touch with the widows. Maybe they're really not hiding anything. Maybe they don't realize that they *do* know something. When the time is right, we'll have a more detailed conversation with them. But I don't think your families are in any danger."

"What if they are?"

"That'll put us in a tough position. We can't send the wolves to protect the sheep. If we have to, we'll get help from outside."

The three men looked at the chief.

"From God or the devil. But I think that the author of the note isn't so much worried about the investigation as he is about the possibility that it might interfere with something already in motion."

Back at the station, Espinosa found a message to call Freire, from the Criminological Institute.

"The three bullets came from the same weapon," Freire said, as soon as he picked up the phone.

"He wasn't worried about using a different gun," Espinosa said. "It's like a signature."

"All we have to do is read it."

Freire's taciturn nature didn't prevent him from being the best forensic researcher on the force, even though his material resources were hardly more extensive than a magnifying glass and he'd been known to pay for more substantial work out of his own pocket.

It was three weeks since the first murder and they still didn't have a single witness. Nobody had seen anything; their informers didn't have a single clue. The silence was absolute. The intended message seemed to have gotten through: anyone who said or hinted at anything was putting themselves at risk.

Espinosa heard the suggestion more than once, in the form of an argument: "Isn't it just corrupt cops killing each other off? Let them kill each other. They're cleaning up the force."

7

Ever since their first encounter in Espinosa's apartment, Irene had always preferred his place. Espinosa visited hers only to pick her up or drop her off, never to spend the night. He didn't mind; her apartment was bigger and magnificently decorated, but his was more relaxing.

As always, Irene arrived with a grocery bag whose contents were predictable, but which she always announced halfway up the stairs.

"Italian bread, smoked salmon, cheeses, wine——"

"If I said the tastiest thing isn't in the bag . . ."

". . . you'd be saying the same thing you said last time."

They hadn't seen each other in a month. They hugged for longer than usual, and Irene was a good hugger, hugging with her whole body; their first kiss was soft at the beginning and then grew more intense; and they sampled each other's bodies before they got to the wine, salmon, and cheese. Irene was a generous lover, offering every part of herself to Espinosa, seeming to enjoy the act even more than her lover did. There was no part of her anatomy Espinosa hadn't visited, but every corner still had inexhaustible secrets that both savored each time they met.

They lay for a while in silence, looking at the ceiling. Espinosa asked the first question:

"Do you still think about Olga?"

"Do you mean do I think about her when we're in bed together or do I remember her sometimes?"

"The second part is rhetorical."

"I still think about her, but not when we're having sex. When we're in bed, I think about you . . . when I can think at all. I think a person's sexuality has a lot of different layers. . . . Old partners are always present; you can't separate lovers that way. But you can be sure of one thing: my favorite part is with you."

Espinosa rolled over, propped himself up with his elbow, and rested his head in his hand. He spent a while looking at her beautiful face and expressive eyes without saying anything.

"What do you want to know?" Irene asked. "If I love you? If I love you more than I loved Olga?"

Espinosa silently looked at Irene, so close that he could hardly bring his eyes to focus on her face.

"They're different loves," Irene continued. "You can't compare it. They're all part of the same love, but I want you to understand that I don't mix them up. You're unique, and I've never loved anyone like I love you. With you, I'm not trying to rebound from anyone. Don't worry."

"I'm not worried. I'm not scared of you or your past. I'm scared of myself."

"Why don't we have a little salmon and a glass of wine to celebrate the present, before going back to bed?"

Espinosa didn't possess Irene's clarity; she could speak so easily about her feelings and emotions. He had a hard time even thinking about his own feelings, much less discussing them. He never knew what to say when introducing Irene to people—"friend" didn't sound right; she wasn't exactly his girlfriend; "lover" . . . nobody introduces someone as their lover. He needed a new vocabulary to describe their relationship. It was like the new kind of family, with its multiple marriages: there still weren't words to describe the various kinds of relationships that resulted.

He ate breakfast alone. Irene had left a note saying that she had to be in São Paulo before lunchtime, and that she had to swing by her house and her office before heading to the airport. She didn't try to act like a wife; even if she were married, she wouldn't fit the stereotype. She also didn't seem like an executive, though she was always on the road for work.

Espinosa was crossing through the Peixoto District on his way to the station when he spotted Welber walking toward him. He immediately understood that the pleasant start to the day would soon be a memory.

"I've been trying to call your cell phone, but you must have forgotten to turn it on."

Espinosa fumbled in his jacket pockets to find the phone, which, like his landline, had been turned off since the night before.

"What's happened this time? For you to come all the way here, after trying to call me . . ."

"I didn't come especially to talk to you, but since your building's on the way I thought you'd like to have a look."

"What happened?"

"A woman. They called saying it was a policewoman. They called the Thirteenth as well, with the same message."

"And is she a cop?"

"No, but she was the mistress of one of the dead ones."

"Which one?"

"Ramos."

"Where was it?"

"Straight ahead, a hundred meters from your building."

"My building?"

"Yeah. Right behind here, on the Rua Santa Clara."

Espinosa took Welber's arm and they turned around and headed back in the direction from which Espinosa had come.

"There's a passageway by my building that goes right to the Rua Santa Clara. Tell me what happened on the way."

"There's not a lot to go on. She was found inside a car, with a bullet in her head, shot point-blank. The murderer was probably sitting in the driver's seat. The car must have been stopped when he fired."

"Have you already been there?"

"I was. There are cops from both precincts."

"What was her name?"

"Rita. Maria Rita. Ramiro saw her yesterday."

"Who found the body?"

"The doorman from the building across the street. He thought it was strange that a woman was sleeping in the car. He went up to it and saw that her shirt was covered with blood."

"When was that?"

"He called at seven-thirty this morning. The station informed Ramiro, who told me to tell you."

The Rua Santa Clara started near the Túnel Velho, wrapped around the Peixoto District, and headed in a straight line to the Avenida Atlântica, cutting Copacabana in half and separating the jurisdictions of the Twelfth and Thirteenth Precincts. There were cars and cops from both at the scene. If it had come down to it, Espinosa could have argued that the crime had occurred on the left side of the street, in his precinct. But the two chiefs and several policemen weren't at the scene to argue about such things. Espinosa lifted the yellow tape blocking off part of the sidewalk. He was recognized and exchanged a few words with some of the other people there, feeling out their mood.

"It looks like killing cops wasn't enough for them and they've decided to try out some terrorism." The comment, made in a raised voice, came from a cop from the Thirteenth, and didn't appear to be directed at anyone in particular. "Serial killer and terrorist." He went on: "You'll see, the son of a bitch killed the woman just to set the tone. Does anyone still doubt that it's a serial killer?" It was clear to Espinosa that the question was directed at him; Welber noticed his boss's discomfort.

"It has nothing to do with you, sir."

"Yes, it does. They know we're investigating, and it's easier for them to go along with the idea that there's some serial killer liquidating cops than to accept that the police force is investigating itself."

"Do you think that's it?"

"That the police force is investigating itself? Maybe. But there's no serial killer. Our murderer isn't choosing the victims, just carrying out orders. Serial killers are American. We don't have those in our culture."

Welber looked at him.

"Crime is also culture," Espinosa concluded.

The detective wasn't sure whether to take the comment seriously.

While Espinosa spoke to some of the policemen individually, Ramiro cased the area. He took in the scene of the crime, examining the car through the windows. Then he paid visits to all the neighboring buildings and spoke with the doormen and garage attendants. He spent most of the morning at the garages of the nearby buildings interrogating employees and residents.

As Espinosa saw it, the crime was of a piece with the preceding ones, with a sole variation: the victim, instead of being a cop, was a cop's mistress. The rest was identical: a single shot, no struggle, no disturbances, no witnesses.

The car had been found with its windows and doors closed but not locked, the key in the ignition. The victim's purse contained money and credit cards, along with personal documents and a cell phone. The car's papers were in the glove compartment.

Cops from the Thirteenth gathered around Espinosa. Almost all of them knew each other, some only by sight, but everyone knew who the chief was and what he was doing there.

"So, sir, any progress in the investigation of our colleagues' deaths?" The question, asked by an old detective from the Thirteenth Precinct, was accompanied by a smile that could have been friendly if it hadn't been delivered with perceptible irony.

"Not much."

"Doesn't it look like a serial killer in the great American tradition?"

"Only if the horse speaks English."

"Huh?"

"Don't worry about it, only kidding."

"What about the people who have been threatening one of your men?"

"It's not exactly a threat. Just a reminder."

"He shouldn't let his guard down. These people aren't messing around."

"People? You think it's more than one?"

"Whoever's doing this"—the older cop pointed to the car—"isn't acting alone."

"Why do you think it's more than one person?"

"Because it would be hard for someone on their own to be that efficient."

"I think exactly the opposite."

"Either way, sir, we've got to be careful. See you later."

The detective was already turning to leave when Espinosa asked, "Speaking of which, when were you talking with the man I've got on the case?"

"I wasn't. I don't even know who's working on it. Why?"

"Because he and I are the only ones who know about the threat."

"Oh, Chief, you know how these things get around."

The detective left without saying anything else. The next person to approach Espinosa was Officer Assunção, whom Espinosa had known since college. He was a friendly guy who patted Espinosa on the shoulder and said, "Well, buddy, what a load of shit, huh? Now they've decided to bump off the wives as well."

"In this case, the mistress," Espinosa answered.

"Same difference."

"It's not exactly the same thing. The wives are still alive."

"Do you think they're in danger?"

"Who? The widows?"

"The mistresses."

"Possibly. This one might have seen something or someone she wasn't supposed to, and the same might go for the others."

"How are we going to cover this up?"

"We're not going to cover it up, we're just not going to tell the press everything. If they ask, tell them someone killed a prostitute. They'll lose interest immediately."

It was early, the sun still low in the sky, but the day was already hot. Espinosa continued to ponder the detective's mention of the threat directed against Ramiro. If they knew about the note, they knew about everything.

Recourse to their usual informers bore no fruit. Many had suddenly disappeared, as if scattered by some supernatural menace; the few that remained claimed total ignorance, and when pressed acted like little girls on the day of their first communion.

Before the day was over, a rumor made its way around the station that some cops were thinking of starting an extraofficial hunt for the killer. That was exactly what Espinosa didn't want. It would trip up the investigations and could easily turn into a witch hunt. Police paranoia was like a viper: it couldn't be stirred up without a violent and uncontrollable reaction. That's why he'd preferred to work with a small group, easier to control and less prone to spectacular bravado. Besides, he was sure that the investigation would depend on little details, not big confrontations. If everybody was on the lookout for a cop killer, it would get so bad that after a few days no one would be able to get near an officer without having a gun pointed at their chest. Espinosa had witnessed similar reactions when the drug lords had threatened to invade police stations to take back their prisoners. At least in that case, the enemy was easily identifiable. The threat now was more terrifying because the enemy was all too familiar, lived in the same house. He was very close by, yet practically invisible.

That night, at home, he ate the leftovers of the night before: a full loaf of Italian bread, pâté, salmon, some cheese, and half a bottle of wine. He took everything into the living room and thought about his night with Irene.

8

With his team busy investigating the double lives of the murdered cops, Welber wasn't around to fend off the reporters, and Espinosa felt particularly exposed to calls like the one he got from the Department of State Security.

". . . and, sir, as for these police murders . . . I'll leave the press to you, since you're the only one who knows anything. When I learn more, I'll be in touch."

"Don't worry about it, I'll take care of them."

"You know how to deal with those people. You manage to get them out of there without the scoop of the year."

"It's not because I'm so efficient; it's because I'm so lazy. I don't like to talk."

"Very good. Right on. I'll have to use that tactic."

Espinosa felt especially uncomfortable that he couldn't name a suspect. It was a struggle between criminal competence and police incompetence. The press was right to be pushy, and cops had every reason to be scared. Yet he didn't see the situation as completely chaotic. It was clear that the person was not killing people at random. The victims had a set profile: second-rate cops who rarely stayed in the same station for long, were relatively unknown, and had never stood out in any way in their profession. The three victims had had double lives, two addresses, two women, and a modest lifestyle, even if their possessions weren't completely modest. So it wasn't just anybody who was being killed. It was the people who, within that pattern, were probably involved in some dangerous business. Since he didn't know what the business was, and since so many cops were involved in shady dealings, there was plenty of reason for other cops to feel threatened. He was sure of one thing: the deaths were not being caused by a supernatural force or by an unknown virus. It was most likely that one person was behind all of them: a hired gun. Espinosa didn't know how many people he'd been hired to kill.

He'd arranged to meet with the group at the end of the morning. Welber was the first to drop by his office to confirm the meeting and find out where it would be held; Artur and Ramiro followed. They decided to meet at the Italian place Espinosa liked, which was a convenient distance from the station. Espinosa was still unsure about the decision to meet outside the office. The idea was to avoid eavesdroppers. But though the measure protected the group from nosy colleagues, it also increased the perception that they were a privileged group.

By twelve-thirty everyone had arrived. They decided to exchange information before eating. Espinosa wasn't expecting big news.

"Ramiro can start, and then Welber and Artur," Espinosa began.

"I still don't know anything about the woman yesterday," Inspector Ramiro began, "except that I'm sure that my interview provoked her murder. It's more than just a coincidence that I talked to her one day and she died the next. We have to protect the other two as quickly as possible. About the three cops, no big news. I spoke with their mistresses this time. Neither the wives nor the mistresses knew much about their business affairs, and they had no idea that the three were working together. It's possible that they once asked where the money was coming from; they probably got a good enough answer to make them lay off the subject. They all agreed that none of the men were on drugs, they weren't drinkers or gamblers, they didn't have any debts, as far as the women knew, and they weren't very outgoing socially. They were good boys. Except they must have forgotten to do their homework."

"Welber, Artur . . ."

"We didn't get much either. Professionally, the three did their jobs, worked on the street. They weren't popular among their colleagues, but they weren't unpopular either. They just avoided people. There's one interesting little quirk in their daily routines: all of them had cell phones, besides the phones in the station, but they often used pay phones in the area. None of their colleagues knew what they did after hours. Another interesting little detail is that none of the cars in their garages were registered in their own names. They seem to have switched cars often."

"It's impossible that they could have kept something so profitable going for so many years without any of their colleagues knowing about it," Espinosa said. "Keep looking. Until we know what business is behind these murders, we won't be able to connect any of the dots. The woman's death is something else to worry about. As soon as we leave here, find the other two and convince them to lie low for a while. I'm afraid that after the mistresses, they'll go after the wives."

The intense summer light was cut by the curtains on the windows, but in spite of the pleasant location and the promise of a tasty meal, Artur tapped his fingers compulsively on the table, while Ramiro tinkered with the toothpicks.

Until the risotto arrived.

After the meal, Ramiro went to Celeste's apartment, on Botafogo Beach. Of the three, she was the most outgoing, and the one with the most comfortable lifestyle. He'd met with her two days before and had been impressed by the good sense she'd shown not only about Nestor but about the police in general. Pretty, young, with a good body, she'd done some cabaret dancing before meeting Nestor, who'd convinced her to leave the theater and help him with his business. He'd said that her intelligence was wasted on an activity that required only her body. While ringing the doorbell, Ramiro thought about her pleasant voice. When, after repeated rings, nobody answered, he went downstairs to look for the doorman.

"I know who you mean, but I'm not sure when I last saw Dona Celeste."

"Have you been here since this morning?"

"That's right, sir."

"And you don't remember having seen her?"

"I don't remember, sir."

"Think about it. She's a pretty woman, hard to miss."

"That's true, but I don't remember, sir."

Ramiro thought the doorman's effort to remember the woman was a little exaggerated: it seemed he was trying more to forget than to remember.

"Has anybody come looking for her in the last few days?"

"Do you mean a man?"

"Man, woman, tortoise, anybody, Jesus! Shall we continue chatting here or go down to the station?"

"No, sir, it's fine here, I just don't remember."

"What time do you get off?"

"Six o'clock, Doctor."

"I'm not a fucking doctor, I'm Inspector Ramiro from the Twelfth Precinct. At six o'clock I'll come back for a talk, and if you haven't remembered anything by then we'll go down to the station to see if we can refresh your memory."

"All I remember is seeing her carrying a suitcase."

"See? You're remembering. The cure is working."

"What . . . ?"

"Was she entering or leaving the building?"

"I think she was leaving."

"And when was this?"

"I think it was yesterday. . . . Yes, yesterday. At the end of the afternoon. I was getting ready to leave."

"Now there's only one more thing before you get back your memory. Before she left with the suitcase, did anybody come in asking for her?"

"That I don't know, Doctor. I can't always see who's in the elevator. People can come in with a resident."

"If you remember anything else, here's my number."

When he left the building, Ramiro was surprised by the contrast between the darkness of the interior and the bright light outside. For a few seconds he looked out at the sailboat-filled Bay of Botafogo with the Sugar Loaf behind it. The beauty of the panorama didn't impress him. What interested him was the view of a few millionaire yachtsmen anchored near the Yacht Club. He turned his back to the view and walked down the Rua São Clemente toward the subway.

The Glória station was four stops after Botafogo. Enough time for Ramiro to think about the questions he was going to pose to Aparecida, the third mistress. He'd never done that before. He usually just let the questions come to him as he was conducting the interview. But in the subway, without a landscape to contemplate through the window, without a friend to talk to, he imagined the meeting he was about to have.

The building was bigger than Celeste's and the doorman just as uncooperative.

A half hour after he arrived, that's how Ramiro put it to Espinosa, Welber, and Artur.

"It was the end of the afternoon when I got to her apartment. I rang her doorbell one, twice, three times, and got no answer. If she was asleep, with her door closed and the air-conditioning on, she wouldn't have heard the bell. I went down and asked the doorman. He said he couldn't be sure about the comings and goings of all the inhabitants, that she was probably home, that she'd left that morning to go to the supermarket, but that she'd come back right afterward and he hadn't seen her leave since then. I went back up and rang again, until I decided to try to open the door. It took no effort: it wasn't locked; all I had to do was turn the knob and it opened. I remembered from my first visit that the door opened directly into the living room and that the hallway to the bedrooms was just to the left. I still thought she was home, especially after what the doorman had said. I slowly opened the door and stuck my head in the direction of the hallway, to try to see if I could hear anything. That was my big mistake. I woke up I don't know how long afterward, with the doorbell ringing in my ear and a terrible headache. I was lying there on the ground and the door was closed. The bell wouldn't stop ringing. I opened the door and met the doorman, who was yelling, asking what I was doing there, who I was, saying he was going to call the police; that's when I realized what had happened. I left him screaming there and went stumbling around the apartment. She was in the bathroom, inside the shower, naked and wet, with a hole in the middle of her chest. The shower was still running. I called you. I didn't let anybody in. The only thing I did besides turning off the shower was grab a plastic bag in the kitchen and fill it with ice."

They were in the living room and the forensic people still hadn't arrived. Ramiro held his ice bag to his head. Espinosa had the doorman come in.

"Good evening. I'm Officer Espinosa from the Twelfth Precinct. I know you're no longer on duty, but we need to ask you a few questions."

"Yes, sir."

"Who was with her in the apartment?"

"Nobody. . . . I mean, I didn't see anybody."

"But you're the doorman?"

"I am, but I can't know everything that goes on."

"Who did you see come into the building this afternoon, besides residents?"

"I only remember him," he said, pointing to Ramiro.

"Besides me!"

"I don't remember anyone, I already told you; I only remember this gentleman."

"What's your name?"

"Waldir, with a *W*."

"Waldir, what happened here was murder. Someone came in, attacked Inspector Ramiro, and killed Dona Aparecida. If we have to, we'll take you down to the station to testify. It'll be very unpleasant, and it will take a lot more time. So stop pretending not to know anything and answer the questions."

"All right."

"Who came to see Dona Aparecida recently?"

"The only man who visits Dona Aparecida is her boyfriend, Mr. Silveira. He's the one who rented the apartment for her. He's a very distinguished man."

"And gives good tips."

"That's not why—"

"Fine, Waldir. Go on."

"Sometimes he gives a gratuity. I help Dona Aparecida whenever she needs it."

"And besides him, who else?"

"Nobody. Sometimes one of the women who lives here, but nobody from outside. Sometimes a girl from her office, but not often."

"And this afternoon you didn't see anybody unknown go up to her floor?"

"No, sir. Sometimes I have to leave for a couple of minutes to go to the bathroom, and I can't see if someone comes in with a resident."

"Fine, Waldir. In any case, you'll have to repeat what you've told me down at the station. If on the way you remember anything, you can add it to your testimony. Welber, take down his full name, address, and the reception area's phone number." Then, turning back to the doorman, Espinosa said, "Now go home and try to remember anything, any unknown man, who might have come in this afternoon. And remember we're dealing with a murder, not something trivial. Any detail, even an insignificant one, could help us find out who killed Dona Aparecida."

"Yes, sir."

"How's your head?" he asked Ramiro.

"On the rocks."

"Did you manage to remember anything? Any detail? If the guy was tall or short, white or black?"

"Chief, I only realized that something had happened when I heard the doorbell clanging like a fire alarm in my head. The guy must have been hiding behind the door. He hit me twice. I must have gone out with the first one. I know it was two because I have bruises in two different places. After knocking me out, he must have gone down the stairs. That's what I think. I didn't see a thing."

"And the third?"

"What third?"

"Weren't there three women?"

"Oh, yes. Her name is Celeste, Nestor's girlfriend. Before I came here, I stopped by her apartment. The doorman said she'd left with a suitcase."

"When was that?"

"Yesterday."

"We should check it out. If she was fleeing to protect herself, it will be hard to track her down."

Espinosa waited for the forensic people to arrive before reporting the death to the morgue and the Forensic Institute. He didn't want anybody else walking around in the apartment.

"Chief," Ramiro went on, "we were the ones who clued the murderer in to these women; we were the ones who caused their deaths. If I hadn't been going around talking to the girls, they'd still be alive."

"We didn't provoke anything. Don't let that ice freeze your brain. You should go home and get some rest."

By the time Welber and Artur left, Freire had already gone over the apartment and left with his collection of plastic envelopes.

The trips Welber and Artur made to Celeste's apartment over the next few days turned up nothing. She hadn't come home.

PART 2

1

She had several dresses spread out over the chair and hanging on her wardrobe's doorknobs. She hadn't yet chosen between white and black, a low-cut dress or a very low-cut dress. Her husband didn't seem to have an opinion; he was more worried about the party thrown in honor of an old friend from Harvard graduate school who was joining the government's economic team. He himself, two years before, had been celebrated at an identical party. Serena thought about how exactly the same all these parties were. Two or three big shots from the government and a bunch of young economists, all convinced that they were the next savior of the fatherland. The moments leading up to the parties, however, were a source of deep pleasure, allowing her to daydream and think. If she entered the party in a transparent dress with nothing underneath, it wouldn't be as exciting for the men there, especially the younger ones, as the announcement of a new economic measure. The women would all have very light skin, very blond hair, and very blue eyes. Anglo-Saxon quality.

She turned around to reconsider the dresses and decided to open the window to see how warm it was outside. The apartment, on the tenth floor of a corner building on the Avenida Atlântica, in Leme, had a living room facing the sea and bedrooms facing a small side street.

The smell of the sea drew her eyes toward the beach. The foam on the waves, lit against the darkness of the night, sparkled almost phosphorescently. She had been looking for a while and was going to close the window when she noticed the commotion in the apartment across the street, less than twenty meters away. A woman was gesticulating and pacing across the room, entering and leaving the visible area framed by the window. She was talking to another person, someone who looked like a man in a cap. Serena couldn't make out what the woman might be saying.

Suddenly, what looked like a purse flew out the window. She saw the strap in the air as the object fell to the ground in the semidarkness of the space between two buildings. She tried in vain to locate it, then turned back to the apartment across the way. She looked back at the sidewalk, waiting for the woman to go down to get the purse, which appeared to be next to the curb, in an area shaded by a tree. She was still trying to discern the purse when a bigger object flew through her visual field, falling to the sidewalk with an impact and a noise that were unmistakable even to someone who had never seen anybody leap off a high building. Serena, horrified, stared at the woman's body on the sidewalk, arms and legs in positions that reminded her of a broken doll. People on the street averted their faces; Serena thought she saw someone take the purse and leave the scene. Almost without moving, her eyes returned to the window across the way. The lights were still on, but nobody was there.

2

Welber and Artur paid several visits to the building on Botafogo Beach, looking for Celeste. According to the doormen, she hadn't come back or been in touch. On Wednesday afternoon, a week after she disappeared, Espinosa doubled back to his office after lunch. Ramiro entered behind him.

"Chief, Celeste called. She wants to talk to you."

"Who answered?"

"I did."

"Why does she want to talk to me? She doesn't know me."

"When I talked to her that time, she said that she knew who you were, that Nestor had mentioned you."

"How did she sound?"

"Confused. She must have been talking from a pay phone, somewhere busy; there was a lot of noise."

"What did she say?"

"She wants to meet you."

"Meet me or talk to me?"

"Both. First, she wanted to talk to you, but since you weren't there——"

"Did she say what she wanted to talk to me about?"

"She said she was scared——"

"Scared of what?"

"She was really nervous, talking fast and sounding disoriented."

"Did you ask her where she was?"

"That was the first thing I asked her. She didn't want to say. She said she doesn't trust the police."

"That's what she said? That she doesn't trust the police?"

"That's right."

"If she doesn't trust the police, why is she calling me at a police station?"

"It was the only number I left for her."

"How did the call end?"

"She hung up abruptly."

"Because of something you said?"

"I don't think so. I just asked her one more time to tell me where she was."

"That's it?"

"I also asked if she needed help."

"And what did she say?"

"She hung up."

"She'll call back. If I'm not here, give her my home number. Don't ask her anything else—she's probably suspicious and scared. Don't forget that she was Nestor's mistress for years; she knows what the police are like and she must have learned to be wary of people, even on the phone."

That night, at home, Espinosa didn't even bother to glance at what was written on the frozen pasta carton: he stuck it in the microwave and went into the living room. Even though he lived alone, he didn't like to eat too casually, sitting on the kitchen counter, staring at the tiles on the wall a few inches from his nose. He took his plate and a can of beer to the table in the living room and sat down in front of the window, gazing out at the lights on the distant hills. He didn't turn on the stereo. He did that only on special occasions, not just to provide background noise. He was used to eating in a hurry, and the first bite revealed a surprise: the pasta was delicious, and it wasn't spaghetti but lasagna. It must have been a survivor from the last time Irene went grocery shopping for him.

From what Ramiro had learned, the possessions of the dead policemen had not been bought all at once but over the years, which indicated that they had a constant, regular source of income, rather than money that had come in a big lump sum. The mistresses were also long-standing acquisitions. They must have witnessed many meetings, participated in many conversations, listened to many confidential exchanges.

Of the three women, Espinosa had seen only two of them, and then only after they were dead. Ramiro had given him a rough description of the survivor, Celeste: young, pretty, smart. She had certainly heard about the deaths of the other two and was making every effort to elude the killer. She probably didn't have much money and, judging from the phone call she'd made to the station, she clearly hadn't left the city. She'd fled her apartment with only a small bag, and someone who leaves like that leaves a lot of things behind. They forget important things, feel that they have to go back but are afraid to . . . and eventually have to ask someone for help—and that's when they slip up. To try to protect her from this possibility, Espinosa asked Welber to get in touch with all her old friends from the time when she was a cabaret dancer.

After finishing the lasagna, he sat in the dusky light of the living room long enough to enjoy two beers. He was still wearing the clothes he'd had on when he came in; all he'd done was empty his pockets and leave his wallet and his gun on his bedroom dresser. That wasn't what he usually did. He almost always took a shower as soon as he got home, but that afternoon, for no particular reason, he had changed his habits. After taking his plate, silverware, and cans back to the kitchen, he went back to the living room, settled into his rocking chair, his favorite, and sat looking a little longer at the buildings across the square and the lights on the hills. He still didn't turn on the stereo, or pick up the book on the coffee table to find out what happened during the hundred and fifty days before the execution. At this rate, the book would unfold in real time. After almost an hour, he realized why he was acting differently this evening: he was waiting for Celeste to call.

She didn't. At eleven o'clock, after he'd showered and stretched out to watch a film on TV, the phone rang, and he answered immediately. It was Welber.

"Sorry about the time, but I thought it was important."

"What happened?"

"I found some of Celeste's colleagues—that is, Carmem Rios's colleagues, her stage name before she met Nestor."

"Where are you?"

"In a bar in Copacabana."

"By yourself?"

"With Artur. We were about to leave when the girls arrived. The show starts at midnight. We had time to talk to them. I got the address of a girl who is still friends with Celeste."

"And?"

"She doesn't do the same show and none of them know what bar she works in now, but they had her address. They said that some big shot in the government keeps her in a fancy apartment. Do you want me to go there now?"

"If she's working in a cabaret, she won't be home now; besides, we don't know who the big shot is. He could make noise about it. We'd better talk to her in the morning."

"They sleep in the morning; after lunch would be better. After *our* lunchtime; they must only eat lunch in the late afternoon."

"Fine. Good work."

3

Serena and Guilherme took the elevator down to the garage, got in the car, and started talking only when they reached the street. They'd been silent ever since she'd agreed, even after what she'd seen, to go to the dinner anyway.

"Look! They still haven't taken the body away. Let's go ask what happened."

They turned the corner and stopped in front of their own building's entrance. Guilherme honked twice, and the doorman came over to the car.

"Yes, sir."

"Sebastião, what happened?"

"The girl threw herself from the tenth floor, sir."

"Did you know her?" Serena asked.

"It looks like she was the cousin of the woman who lives in 1002. I didn't get close enough to see, but that's what the doorman over there told me."

"And the purse? I saw they took her purse."

"Nobody said anything about a purse, Dona Serena."

"But there was a purse . . . it was thrown out of the window, I saw it."

The husband put his hand on his wife's shoulder as he thanked the doorman and pushed the button to roll up the window.

"Let's go, darling."

"Guilherme, I saw the purse get thrown out of the window! Just like I saw, afterward . . ."

"But it won't do you any good to talk about this with the doorman. It won't do you any good to talk to anyone, except maybe the police, and I don't think you'd want to do that."

"Why not?"

"Because it's just asking for trouble."

"Strange, your idea of being a good citizen."

"Sweetie, this isn't Washington."

"Just our luck."

The dinner wasn't as unpleasant as she had feared, and the women weren't as blond or blue-eyed as the ones at the earlier party. The only person who was uninteresting and off-putting was Serena herself. The beauty and sensuality that so charmed men were undercut by her glum silence.

The next morning she looked for some news about the suicide. She told the maid to go buy the tabloids, which were most likely to cover violent events. There wasn't a single reference. After breakfast, she put on a jogging outfit, to make it look like she was going to run down the Avenida Atlântica, and stopped off to see the other building's doorman. With the newspaper under her arm, she struck up a conversation. He was used to seeing her every time she left her apartment on foot.

"Good morning."

"Morning, ma'am."

"There wasn't anything in the papers about the girl."

"Oh, well, it wasn't supposed to be."

"Why not?"

"The doctor wouldn't let them."

"What doctor?"

"Dr. Eliezer, the owner of the apartment."

"Eliezer who?"

"I don't know, ma'am, I just know his name is Dr. Eliezer."

"So Dr. Eliezer's really as powerful as all that?"

"I don't know if he's powerful, but people seem to do what he says."

"Right. And he was the one with the girl when she fell?"

"Nobody was with the girl; she was by herself."

"Are you sure?"

"As sure as I am that you're standing here."

"What about her purse?"

"What?"

"The purse that fell with her."

"There wasn't a purse, no, ma'am."

"Oh, then I was wrong. I thought I saw a purse."

"The only thing that fell was the girl."

"May she rest in peace."

"Amen."

"See you later."

"Good-bye, ma'am."

Serena dumped the paper in the first trash can and, instead of crossing the Avenida Atlântica, decided to go back home. She could think better on a sofa than walking down the street, where there were too many distractions, starting with the sea itself. She didn't take off her shorts or her tennis shoes and went straight to her husband's home office. She sat at the desk, pushed his computer aside, took a few pieces of paper and a pencil, and began writing.

An hour later, she'd come up with a list of names and questions, as well as some charts and a rough sketch of the falling purse and woman. After she'd tossed a few pages into the wastebasket, she was startled by her own conclusion: the woman hadn't killed herself or fallen accidentally.

She told Guilherme what she thought had happened.

"Serena, this doesn't make any sense," he said. "The cops were there, they talked to the people, went over the apartment, and everyone agrees that the woman threw herself out the window, and now you're saying she was murdered. This is really serious. Nobody makes an accusation like that without serious consequences."

"I'm not saying I'm sure it was murder. I'm simply suggesting to the police, who, after all, weren't there very long, that there might have been more to it."

"But you can't just suggest things after a forensic examination has been done. This is no joke, Serena."

Serena fell silent once more. She wouldn't mention again what she'd seen from the window. The woman must have been about her age, and she'd decided that she wouldn't let the "doctor," whoever he was, arrange matters for his own convenience.

Around noon, she noticed, from her dressing room, movement in the apartment across the way. There were several men in work uniforms, and on the street a little moving van was parked next to the sidewalk. Over the next few hours she returned to her observation post several times, until she was sure that the van was gone and nobody was left in the apartment. At the end of the afternoon another set of men arrived. There was no truck on the street. Just before dinner, when she was getting ready to sit down to eat, she saw lights in the apartment and men with ladders and paint rollers, painting the walls. She didn't mention it during dinner.

"Are you still thinking about the accident last night?"

"Of course not. Besides, as the saying goes, 'A problem you can't solve is already solved.'"

"That's better. There's really nothing you can do about it."

When she went to change into her nightgown, the men were still painting the apartment. She slept fitfully and woke up twice during the night. Both times she went to her dressing room. The lights were still on in the other apartment.

She didn't have a gun at home. If the murderer came back for her, she would need to be able to defend herself, even though she'd never fired a gun in her life. Guilherme would think the idea of buying a revolver absurd, but he'd think it was even more absurd to buy a revolver for a danger he considered sheer fantasy.

In the morning, there was nothing at all happening in the apartment across the way.

Even though he lived on the Avenida Atlântica, Guilherme Afonso Rodes had never set foot on the sands of Copacabana Beach. Since childhood he'd only gone to pools at
exclusive clubs, and when he ventured into salt water, it
was on beaches in the Mediterranean. He'd been raised to
think of public places as probable sources of parasitic infec-
tions. Foreign beaches were different. He'd learned to read
in English; for years, when he had to do simple mathemat-
ical operations in his head, he did them in English rather
than Portuguese. That was why everyone was so shocked
by the announcement of his engagement and marriage to
Serena. But, contrary to his family's expectations, he hadn't
so much changed Serena as Serena had transformed Guilherme Afonso Rodes's bureaucratic mind. In his world,
prudence reigned; Guilherme's newfound willingness to
live a little more on the wild side was the result of a spell
cast by the witch Serena.

Sunday was her husband's golf day—the sport the new
finance minister favored—and Serena could focus on her
research without interruptions. With the classified sections
of every paper opened on the dining room table, she looked
at the lists of apartments for rent and sale. She searched by
neighborhood, type of building, price. She looked one more
time through the real estate ads for Leme. Nothing. Maybe
they hadn't finished painting it yet; maybe they were
checking the electrical wires and the plumbing; maybe
he'd decided to let it sit for a while: people don't like to live
in an apartment where someone killed themselves. The
soul might not yet have found peace, and could return to

disturb the new residents. For whatever reason, the apartment wasn't listed for rent or sale.

She put on her shorts, T-shirt, and tennis shoes and went downstairs. It was almost noon, and the heat was insufferable. She crossed the street and found the doorman.

"Hi there."

"Good morning, ma'am."

"Do you know if the doctor is trying to rent the apartment? I have a friend who's looking for a place."

"Oh, ma'am, he's trying to rent it out short-term."

"Is it already taken?"

"Not yet. Maybe he'll rent it longer-term."

"Right, maybe. . . . Anyway, thanks a lot."

"No problem, ma'am."

There was no doubt about it. They were wiping out the traces, making it impossible for her to examine the apartment for clues. This only made Serena more certain that it hadn't been a suicide. She went back home and sat looking out her dressing room window, trying to conjure up the scene she'd witnessed.

After half an hour, Guilherme called from the club, asking if she wanted to meet him for lunch.

"It could be right here, at the club. If you want, I'll send the driver to pick you up."

"No, honey, it's too hot and I'd rather stay home; I'm trying to tie up some loose ends around here."

"All right. Take care."

"You too."

In the phone book, she found the number of the police and asked for the station that included Leme.

"Twelfth Precinct, ma'am, Rua Hilário de Gouveia."

She took down the address and phone number. She thought that the best day to call would be Monday, a normal working day. Policemen must also want a break on Sundays.

4

Friday night's suicide was mentioned to Espinosa only on Monday morning, when the body, after being autopsied, was released to the family.

"Who went to the scene?"

"Ferreira. He was on duty at the time."

"Who went with him?"

"Nobody. He went alone. It was dinnertime and he——"

"Ferreira didn't talk to any witnesses?"

"They said there was no need to."

"What do you mean there was no need to?! A woman falls from the tenth floor of a residential building and the policeman in charge of the investigation doesn't think he needs to talk to anybody?"

"It seems he got instructions——"

"He got instructions?!"

The dialogue between Espinosa and Ramiro took place in the chief's office.

On the intercom the officer ordered Detective Ferreira to come to his office while Ramiro tried, without much conviction, to soften the blows the detective was about to receive.

"Chief, Ferreira isn't very smart. He seems to have gotten a phone call from some authority, he got scared——"

"What authority?"

"I'm not sure; it seems to have come from the palace."

"Palace? What fucking palace?"

Ferreira came in at that exact moment.

"Hello, Chief. You called me?"

"Yes, I did. Why didn't you take anybody's testimony in the case of the woman who killed herself?"

"I talked to a few people, sir, and went to the victim's apartment, but as soon as I came downstairs an officer from the car that answered the call said that someone wanted to talk to me and handed me a cell phone. It was the secretary's office, notifying us that since it was obviously a suicide there was no need to investigate more extensively. That the woman was alone at the time, there were no signs of violence, that everything was fine and it was time to turn the page. I don't know how they knew that, but it was true, I saw it myself. The man on the phone said there was no need to open an investigation."

"Who was the man?"

"The doctor who called from the office of the secretary."

"And you forgot the name of the doctor?"

"He was talking from the office. I'm not sure if it was the office of the secretary or the Cabinet of the governor or what; he said a lot of things and mentioned a lot of names, he said he knew you, he told me not to bother you so late at night, that they'd take care of everything."

"And the woman, who was she?"

"What woman, sir?"

"The dead woman, dumbass!"

"It was the cousin of the woman who lived in the apartment."

"And the cousin of the woman who lived in the apartment doesn't have a name?"

"Nobody knew."

"What do you mean, nobody knew? The woman didn't know her cousin's name?"

"She must know it, sir, but she disappeared."

"She disappeared?"

"That's right."

"And the name of the resident, you don't know that either?"

"Her name is Dona Rosita, sir. She's the protégée of some big shot. Apparently he was in a meeting with the governor when the woman threw herself out of the window."

"Which explains how the body has already been autopsied and buried."

"But there's no doubt it was a suicide, Chief. She was alone in the apartment. And they say she was really depressed and having all sorts of problems, taking pills, that sort of thing."

"Who's 'they'? The chief or his deputy?"

"That's what he said on the phone."

"We're going to open an investigation—"

"But the—"

"Not forever. Go to the Forensic Institute and get a copy of the autopsy report. If the report's not ready yet, talk to the guy who's doing it and ask him what he found out. I want to know if the victim was on drugs, what kind of medication she was taking, anything you can get out of him. Don't forget the name of the family member who collected the body."

That same afternoon, Welber and Artur went to Celeste's friend Rosita's address, the one they had gotten from the girls at the club. It was an old building in Leme, with small apartments, a few feet from the Avenida Atlântica. Even though she hadn't worked with Celeste recently, there was the possibility that Celeste would stop by looking for her, and the cops were hoping that was the case. When they flashed their badges, they were met with a helpfulness rarely encountered by policemen from doormen.

"The doctor said you gentlemen were coming over."

Welber thought it best not to ask what doctor the guy was talking about. The detectives also had no idea how the "doctor" knew that they were coming over, or why he'd told the doorman to cooperate.

"Could you please tell Dona Rosita that we're here?"

"Dona Rosita?"

"That's right."

"But Dona Rosita isn't here."

"Did she go out?"

"You people don't know?" The exchange of "gentlemen" for "people" was accompanied by a sudden chill in the doorman's tone.

"We don't know what?"

"Who are you? Weren't you sent by the doctor?"

"We certainly were sent by the doctor, here's our ID. But what we don't know is if our doctor is the same as yours. Ours is the chief of the Twelfth Precinct, which is all you need to know. Now please tell me if Dona Rosita is home."

"Dona Rosita disappeared as soon as her cousin threw herself out the window."

"What?"

"Her cousin threw herself out of the window, on Friday."

Welber and Artur tried to keep their cool, but they were too shocked to act indifferent.

"Fuck, Ferreira's case!"

"What's Ferreira's case?" the doorman asked.

"Who was the woman?"

"I already told you. It was Dona Rosita's cousin. She came here a few days ago."

"What was her name?"

"I think it was Ângela."

"And what did she look like?"

"She was really pretty too; they looked more like sisters than cousins."

"Did you see her body?"

"I'm not like some people, who do everything but stick their fingers in the corpse—"

"And Dona Rosita, what happened to her?"

"She disappeared. She didn't even wait to see her

cousin's body. She didn't even come get her things. It seems the doctor told her to spend a few days away. To forget."

"Did Dona Rosita live alone?"

"She did. The doctor doesn't want anyone living with her. The apartment belongs to him and he supports her, but they don't live together. He has a family."

"Did she ever have visitors?"

"What do you mean?"

"Visitors. Did she have friends who visited her?"

"Not men. The doctor wouldn't like that. Sometimes a girlfriend would come over. The doctor didn't like that either, but he let her. Like this girl. Except she wasn't a friend, she was her cousin."

"The cousin was alone when she fell?"

"She was, I think she was; I had just come on. I start at eight, and the thing happened around nine. I didn't see when she came in. I don't know if she left. She rarely left the house."

"Who came here afterward?"

"First the cops in a police car, then a cop on foot, then two others, in coats and ties, who work in the palace; they took care of everything. It didn't take long for a car to come take away the body. The men in coats and ties stayed more than an hour up in the apartment. They left with a suitcase."

"And then the doctor sent you a nice fat tip."

The doorman looked at the two cops silently.

"Are we going up?" Artur asked Welber.

"I can't imagine the doctor's men left anything. Let's go. The chief needs to know about this immediately."

The weekend had passed without a call from Irene, despite the messages he'd left on her machine; the fact didn't lift his spirits on this hot Monday morning. Espinosa walked slowly, on the shady side of the street, on his way to the station.

"Sir, you got here right on time. There's a woman on the phone who wants to talk to you. She won't give her name and she won't speak to anybody else. She's on the line now."

"Put her through."

Celeste would have called his apartment. He ran up two flights of stairs faster than he'd planned to and sweatily answered the phone.

"Hello, Espinosa speaking."

"Sir, I have an important piece of information."

"Thank you. Who's speaking?"

"Let's leave my name for later; the important thing is what I have to say."

"Go ahead, ma'am."

"I'd rather not say over the phone."

"We can talk here at the station."

"I'd rather not do that either, sir. Can't we meet somewhere else?"

"You have to admit it's not very reasonable to ask a police chief to leave the station to meet someone who claims to have an important piece of information but won't confide the nature of the information, especially when the person won't come to the station or give her name."

"You're right, sir, but I can tell you that the reason I'm calling concerns the woman who fell from the tenth floor of a building in Leme on Friday night."

"I know what you're talking about, the girl who killed herself."

"That's the point, sir. She didn't kill herself."

"Where are you calling from?"

"From a pay phone, by the victim's building."

"I can meet you at that corner at noon. Is that all right?"

"I'll be waiting."

"I'll be in a taxi. I'll get out carrying a coat in my hand."

In that part of Leme, the blocks were long but narrow, so that at the place the woman named there was only one building on each side of the street. Espinosa saw a woman leave the lobby of the building opposite and cross the street.

There was no doubt that it was the woman he'd seen a month before in a café downtown.

Her face looked well rested, her hair was well coiffed, and even the little lines around her mouth and eyes had almost completely disappeared. She really was beautiful, even without the provocative skirt, or the shorts she was now wearing.

"I'm sorry to be hiding behind the doorman, but I didn't

know who was going to show up. My name is Serena Rodes."

"I'm Chief Espinosa from the Twelfth Precinct."

"Thank you so much for your kindness, sir. I didn't want anyone to listen in. I'm not sure the phone is safe, and a police station is too public. Maybe my secret isn't a secret from anyone else . . ."

Espinosa awaited some sign that she recognized him: a twitch of the eyebrows, a slower gaze . . . but there was nothing. She was seeing him for the first time.

"We'd better have a seat while we talk," Espinosa said, looking around.

"Of course, sorry. There's a restaurant with sidewalk tables right around the corner."

Serena was dressed as if she'd come downstairs to buy a magazine from the kiosk—Bermuda shorts, T-shirt, and tennis shoes—but even so she was as seductive as when she'd worn the skirt with a slit up the side. It was even hotter than it had been when he'd left home to go to the station. They sat beneath an enormous umbrella, at a table protected from beggars and street vendors, and ordered fruit juice, the only reasonable drink in that temperature. The few clouds looked tacked onto the blue sky. Even right next to the beach, there was not the slightest breeze.

"Why did you hide in the entrance of your building?"

"I'd never seen a police chief before."

"What did you expect?"

"I don't know, but someone different."

"And what made you leave your hiding place?"

"You look normal. I'm sorry, I've never seen someone like you before, but I've heard a lot of stories."

"Do you mean I passed the test?"

"I'm never wrong about people, at least about the essentials."

"So can I hear your story?"

"Of course. And once again, thanks for coming."

Without dramatizing it, Serena gave him a detailed account of what she'd seen from her window and the conversations she'd had with the doorman, including the one the day before about renting the apartment.

Espinosa waited for her to finish before asking any questions.

"Are you sure about the purse? Couldn't it have been a piece of paper blown by the wind, or a piece of clothing?"

"It was clearly a purse, the kind with a long strap, and I could see it perfectly."

"Did you ever see the other person inside the apartment?"

"Only briefly. Not enough to really say anything."

"Man or woman?"

"It looked like a man."

"Why do you think they were fighting instead of just talking?"

"Because she looked so worked up. I couldn't see much; it was all very quick."

"You said on the phone that you had your doubts about her death."

"Not about the death—about the fact that everyone's calling it a suicide."

"Why do you doubt it?"

"Sir, nobody who's going to kill themselves throws their purse out first. It doesn't make sense. It's like a person who's about to throw themselves in front of a moving car throwing their purse first."

"She couldn't have fallen together with the purse?"

"No! I saw the purse falling. I didn't see the woman. The purse fell first."

"A person who's about to commit suicide can do strange things."

"And what about the guy who was with her? Why didn't he stop her? Why did he disappear?"

"What do you think?"

"I think he disappeared because he was the one who pushed her. It wasn't suicide, Officer, it was murder."

"And is that why you're being so careful about meeting me?"

"Absolutely. I'm scared. The murderer saw me through the window."

"You're very confident that it was a murder."

"Sir, that's the only reason we're sitting here."

"What I meant was that the elements you've given me are very valuable for my investigation, but they're still a little too fragile to draw any conclusions."

"But I saw—"

"I'm going to tell you a story, Dona Serena. One morning, many years ago, in the city of Venice, a baker was making bread when he heard a scream followed by the sound of things falling at the back of his bakery. When he opened the door to look, he saw a man lying in the street with a knife in his stomach. He ran to help him and was taking out the knife when the woman next door, attracted by the noise, opened the window and saw a man lying in a puddle of blood in the street and another above him, holding a knife. The baker was arrested, tried, and convicted, thanks to the woman who saw him stabbing the victim."

"I understand. But can we do anything?"

"First, we have to find out who the man is you saw in the apartment. Then we have to make sure he wasn't trying to help the woman, like the unfortunate baker."

"It looked like they were fighting."

"The man might have been trying to convince her not to do anything extreme."

"You think that's what it was?"

"No, but I can't eliminate the possibility."

Serena gestured as she spoke. As she moved her arms the movement of her white cotton T-shirt made it clear that she wasn't wearing a bra. It was so hypnotic that it was difficult for Espinosa to stay focused on her face rather than the enchanting swaying of the breasts in front of him.

Serena sat looking at Espinosa for a while, but he felt that she was looking right through him, trying to focus on some undefined place beyond him. There was nothing out of the ordinary about her brown eye color, but her gaze ranged from sugary sweet to piercing and metallic, with every nuance in between. Her face expressed her feelings perfectly.

"Well, I hope I haven't taken up your time unnecessarily. Maybe I'm overdoing it."

"Don't worry about that. I'm really glad you told me."

The conversation had arrived at its end. Espinosa thought that any attempt to stretch it out would be awkward, even though he could have talked to a woman like that all day. He left enough money on the table to cover the juices, and both of them got up at the same time. There were still a few feet between the restaurant and the entrance to her building, enough for them to talk about the heat and the unsuitability of tropical clothing. Before he left, they exchanged phone numbers.

Instead of getting in a cab and heading back to the station, Espinosa crossed the street and went looking for the doorman of the other building. It wasn't the same one who had been there on the night of the accident, and he took Espinosa for someone looking to rent the apartment. Espinosa didn't correct the mistake.

"I don't know how much the rent is; you'd have to ask the agent. Here's the phone number."

"Isn't there some story about a woman killing herself in the apartment?"

"No, sir, nobody killed themselves in the apartment. A woman died, but on the sidewalk, over where that car is parked."

"She was killed on the sidewalk?"

"No, she fell."

"Fell?"

"Yeah. Fell."

"Just like that, walking along, she dropped dead?"

"No, sir, she fell from up there."

"From the tenth floor?"

"They say when that happens the person dies before they hit the ground."

"Sometimes."

luiz alfredo garcia-roza

"But it's a nice apartment and a great neighborhood. You'll really like it."

Espinosa took down the real estate agent's phone number and looked up at the dead woman's apartment. He also looked back at Serena's apartment. Nobody at the window.

Despite the visit to the restaurant, he still hadn't eaten. He went back, sat in the same place, and asked the same waiter for their most popular sandwich and a beer. He wasn't yet ready to return to the station. There were too many questions. The coincidences were the most intriguing part. The coincidence of the two meetings—seeing her at the café downtown and then interviewing her as a witness—plus the coincidence that the victim lived right across from her and the coincidence that Serena was in the only room in the house that faced the victim's apartment at precisely the time the woman fell. . . . His other questions concerned Serena's story itself. Had there actually been a purse thrown out of the window before the woman fell? Had there really been someone else in the apartment and had the victim been fighting with that person? If she had been tossed out the window, why hadn't she screamed? Why hadn't she tried to defend herself?

From where he was, near the great Rock of Leme, the view of the Avenida Atlântica was very different from the one he was used to. The elegant curve of the beach was completely visible, up to Copacabana Fort. He'd had better sandwiches, the heat was still intense, but the beer was just the right temperature. He sat a few more minutes taking

100

in the view and thinking about Serena before finally heading back to work.

It was only near the end of the afternoon, when Welber
and Artur returned to the station, that the two stories
merged into one.

"Chief, the address of the woman who threw herself out
of the window of the tenth floor of that building in Leme
was the same as Celeste's friend Rosita. We managed to get
the doorman to reveal that the dead woman was a cousin
who had been staying at Rosita's apartment for the past
few days. It must have been Celeste."

Espinosa asked them to repeat the story one more time.
As soon as the detectives finished, Espinosa thought for a
few seconds in silence, then told them about his meeting
with Serena Rodes.

"It might not have been a suicide," Espinosa said.

"Murder?"

"It's possible."

"So the guy managed to get rid of the cops and the mistresses."

"If it was the same killer."

"Do you think there could be more than one?"

"Maybe. Of the six deaths, Celeste's was different. Even
the ambiguity: was it suicide or murder?"

At the end of the day, before Espinosa went home, Detective Ferreira arrived from the Forensic Institute. Espinosa was alone in his office.

"Good afternoon, Chief. I went back to the Forensic Institute. I'd already been there on Saturday morning."

"What did you get?"

"There's something strange, Officer. The name of the woman who died is the same as the woman who lived there, Rosita."

"What do you mean?"

"The name of the woman they did the autopsy on was Rosa Maria do Nascimento, known as Rosita."

"Are you sure?"

"Absolutely. I talked with the guy in charge of IDs and the one who autopsied her."

"Call Welber, Artur, and Ramiro."

The first two were still in the station; Ramiro had gone home.

"They killed the wrong woman," Espinosa said as soon as his colleagues came in.

"What?"

"That's right. They killed the wrong woman."

"It wasn't Celeste?"

"No. It was her friend."

"How could the murderer have mixed them up?"

"I don't think he mixed them up, I just don't think he knew what she looked like. He probably had an address, a name, and a description, but no photo. Celeste and the friend were the same age and, according to the doorman, looked a lot alike."

"And the doorman, how could he have gotten it wrong?"

"He only saw the body from a distance."

"But the 'doctor's' men didn't get it wrong."

"Of course not. That's why they cleared the apartment

out so quickly. As soon as the doctor learned that the dead woman was his girlfriend, he had them take everything out of the apartment and arranged for the autopsy and burial."

"That means Celeste is still alive."

"She must have gotten there right when her friend fell. She must be hiding, scared."

"In that case, the murderer doesn't know he killed the wrong woman."

"He knows, if he managed to get the purse."

"Why would someone who was being threatened like that throw her purse out of the window?"

"For either one of two reasons: to attract attention from people outside or—"

Just then the phone on Espinosa's desk rang. He let it ring once, twice, three times; on the fourth ring, Welber took the phone off the hook and held it up.

"Or . . . ?"

"So the murderer couldn't see what was in the purse."

"And what was in the purse?"

"Her ID."

Welber handed the phone to Espinosa and sat looking at him until Espinosa had finished speaking and hung up.

"It must have happened like this," Espinosa went on. "The murderer discovers where Celeste is hiding. Doesn't matter how. He gets into the building without being seen and rings her doorbell. Rosita answers. He knows that there are two women in the apartment, and the description he has matches the woman who opens the door. Since the other woman isn't home, he has to make sure that she's the one he's looking for. That's when he makes a mistake: he asks her name. Rosita, realizing that he doesn't know what Celeste looks like, figures they're both safe as long as he doesn't find out. He keeps asking. They start fighting. That's when he sees her purse. She grabs it before he gets to it. He tries to yank it away from her, but she throws it out the window first. Even though he's not sure who she is, he's already revealed himself to be the murderer, so he pushes her to her death."

"And what happened to the purse?"

"He—or some pedestrian—took advantage of the confusion to snatch it from the sidewalk. Celeste must have come in right then and noticed what happened, then ran away without even collecting her things from the apartment."

6

Serena was used to eating alone. That day, however, her husband had decided to have dinner at home, and she thought that it was the right time to mention her meeting with Officer Espinosa. She still had a clear image of Espinosa in her mind, but she couldn't remember what color his eyes were. He was a pretty attractive man. She suspected that she'd overstepped some boundary, but she wasn't sure exactly which one. She felt as if she'd committed adultery.

As soon as her husband walked in the door, before he could even start in about the problems at the Ministry of Finance, Serena took the initiative.

"I spoke to Chief Espinosa today."

"What?"

"I saw the chief of the Twelfth Precinct today."

"You went to the station to talk about the woman who killed herself?"

"I didn't go to the station . . . and she didn't kill herself."

"My God, Serena, what's going on?"

"What's going on is that I'm not going to pretend that I'm blind or retarded."

"Who is this guy, and what did you say to him?"

"His name is Espinosa, he's very polite and calm, and he came here to talk to me."

"He came here to our house?"

"No, he came here to Leme. He didn't want to, he wanted me to go over to the station, but when I said that it was about the woman they said threw herself out of the tenth-floor window he asked where I was calling from. I said a public phone and he suggested we meet at noon. We talked at one of the tables on the sidewalk at the place around the corner. The police didn't know there was someone else in the apartment and they didn't know anything about the purse."

"Serena, I'm sure all of this is true, but I don't understand why you're getting involved. The chief can't pretend you haven't spoken to him, and now you're part of a police investigation."

"Worse things have happened to me."

"No, they haven't, Serena. You don't know what you've gotten yourself into."

"It would have been worse if I hadn't gotten involved."

"I can see if I can't help the officer forget he talked to you."

"So if you can't shut me up, you'll try to shut him up."

"No, Serena, I'm trying to keep you out of trouble."

"Let's just pretend that a woman, our neighbor, who was my age, wasn't thrown out of a window in front of ours and didn't die crushed on the sidewalk. And you think you're going to fix the whole country."

"I'm an economist, not a policeman."

"Lucky for the police."

Guilherme still had his jacket on; they were still in the

living room, where he had gone to drop his briefcase after he'd walked in the door. They were both standing, but while Serena had stayed fixed in the same position, he had been pacing the room during the conversation. His steps were deliberate; he had his hands in his pockets, and when he spoke it was calmly. But Serena knew that the calmer he looked, the closer he was to an explosion. That wasn't what she wanted. All she wanted was to be able to talk about the subject that was tormenting her with the same energy with which they discussed her husband's problems at the ministry. She sat down on the sofa and tried to relax. She was still wearing the same clothes she'd worn at lunch, and she was still as excited as when she'd said good-bye to the officer.

Espinosa left the office earlier than usual. He was sure that Celeste would try to reach him at home. He also wanted to think about his meeting with Serena. There was no doubt about it: she was the same woman he'd seen downtown. She hadn't shown any sign of recognizing him, and there was no reason why she should. She'd been the one who'd come into the café, and he'd been just a guy sitting there drinking a cappuccino. No reason why she should have noticed him.

It was still light outside when he headed down the Avenida Copacabana, turned right, walked for two blocks, then cut through the Galeria Menescal, which connected the Avenida Copacabana to the Rua Barata Ribeiro. He could have reached the Peixoto District by taking a right out of the station; it was less than half the distance. But he wouldn't have passed by the Arabic take-out place in the Galeria Menescal.

He was walking into the Galeria, dividing his thoughts between the Arabic food and Serena, when he felt a tap on his arm.

"Officer Espinosa?"

He didn't have to ask the woman's name. The frightened look was introduction enough.

"I'm Celeste."

The gallery was wide, with shops on both sides, and lots of people passed through it. It was this last bit that worried Espinosa. He put his arm around Celeste's shoulders as if they were old friends, and the two walked toward the Arabic restaurant.

"Sorry, I followed you from the station. I was looking for a more populated place to approach you."

"It's dangerous for you here."

"I don't know where else to go. I left everything I had behind me. Did you see what they did to my friend?"

"I did."

"The son of a bitch thought it was me."

"You can't expose yourself. They could be following you."

"I don't think so. They lost my scent. I didn't go back to my place or my friend's."

At the restaurant, Espinosa sat between the gallery and

Celeste. If they were going to try anything against her they'd have to get close, and his eyes were peeled.

"Let's eat something here, like old friends. The murderer doesn't know exactly what you look like. Do you want some falafel?"

"Sure."

He ordered two falafels and two soft drinks.

"You have to hide."

"I don't have anywhere to go. Ever since they killed Rosita, I've been staying in a little hotel near here, but my money won't hold out for long. All I have are the clothes on my back. I need to buy some stuff. I used my ATM card to take out all the money I had in the bank. It wasn't much, but I took out a little bit every day. I didn't want to go to my own branch."

The weak lighting of the gallery was augmented by the bright lights of the shops, but it was still difficult to make out people a little distance off, especially at dusk, when the light was weakest.

"I don't think it's safe for us here. You might not be being followed, but I might well be."

"Where should we go?"

"Let's leave on the Barata Ribeiro side. You hang on to my arm. As soon as we see a taxi, we'll jump in. If anybody's following me, they'll know I live two blocks from here, and they won't be expecting to see me get into a taxi."

"And then?"

"I don't know yet."

They walked nearly half a block before they found an empty taxi. As soon as the driver hit the gas pedal, they both looked back to see if anyone was waving desperately for another cab. They didn't see anything suspicious.

"Now that they might have seen us together, my apartment isn't safe for you. Where's your hotel?"

"A few feet from your building."

"What?"

"It's also in the Peixoto District."

"I know which one you're talking about. I had to stay there once when my apartment was being painted. Was it a coincidence?"

"What?"

"That you chose a hotel right near my house."

"I know where you live, sir. I have Nestor's address book."

"Can I make a suggestion? Since we're already holding hands, you can stop calling me sir."

Celeste jerked back and removed her hand from Espinosa's arm.

"Sorry—it's the first time in the last few days that I've felt safe. I just didn't want that feeling to end."

"You'll still be safe."

Espinosa told the driver to turn around after three or four blocks. He took the Avenida Copacabana back in the opposite direction, and turned onto Figueiredo Magalhães, stopping almost at the end, near the Túnel Velho. They got out and waited for the taxi to drive off, then stood there on the sidewalk for a while to make sure no other car had stopped nearby. Convinced they hadn't been followed, they walked the few hundred yards to the back entrance to the Peixoto District, a little alley used only by locals. The Hotel Santa Clara was located on one of the side streets in the neighborhood, indistinguishable from the other three-story colonial-style buildings. When they reached the reception area, it was already getting dark.

"Does anybody know you're here?"

"Nobody."

"What name are you using?"

"Ângela Cardoso."

"Even if they've seen us together, they can't know about this place. You'll be fine here if you're careful. Don't leave unless it's absolutely necessary. It's best if you don't leave at all. When I want to talk to you, I'll use the name Benedito. Don't answer calls from anybody else. Remember: I'll never use the name Espinosa. I'll only be Benedito."

"Is that your first name?"

"Almost. I'll get you some clothes. Do you need to leave to eat?"

"No, I've been cooking here."

"That's better. Now listen. I'm not going to come back here. If you absolutely need to speak with me, call my house and leave the name Ângela on the machine. I'll call you from another phone."

"Espinosa . . . he threw my friend out of the window, right?"

"So it seems. I'm very sorry."

111

Celeste kissed Espinosa on both cheeks and went in.

The distance from the hotel to Espinosa's building was only a couple hundred feet. As soon as he got home, he checked his messages. There was one: "Hey, hon. If you're not chasing after too many criminals, maybe I could bring something over for dinner."

He called Irene. "Do you want me to come get you?"

"Not necessary."

"Irene, I need a favor. Would you have a couple of simple dresses that you could bear to part with?"

"As long as they're not for you, I can check. What size?"

"It must be the same as yours."

"Hmm. Is that just a guess?"

"Right."

"I'll see what I can do. I'll be there in an hour."

While he was in the shower, Espinosa thought about what an exceptional woman Irene was. If he had asked his ex-wife the same question, it would have been greeted with a bunch of snippy comments, even if she knew they were unjustified. Irene would never put herself in the position of being a nag.

She arrived an hour later, carrying a bag with bread, cold cuts, and wine in one hand; in the other, covered in plastic, were some clothes. Espinosa went down to help her as soon as she buzzed.

As they walked upstairs, Irene described the food she'd brought, and when they went into the apartment she laid the clothes out on the sofa.

"If it's what I think, I decided the girl would need underpants as well. Everything I brought is easy to wash and doesn't even need to be ironed. I saw you on TV the other day. I thought you were hiding someone."

"In fact, she was hiding at a friend's house. The friend got killed. The murderer mixed them up, and now he's after her."

"Is she here?"

"No. I'm the only one who knows where she is, and it's better that way. Nobody else can get in trouble."

"Except you."

"That's what I get paid for."

"Which doesn't mean . . ."

"Of course not."

"Do you think the murderer could find her?"

"When he killed her friend, he eliminated his only way of finding her. Now, he's back to the drawing board."

"He could start with you."

"There's nothing to tie me directly to the girl, and I'm sure nobody followed us to the place she's hiding."

"So you think she's safe?"

"For a few days."

"Why only for a few days?"

"They know what they're doing. They've already killed three cops and three women right under our noses, without leaving a single clue. We don't have any idea who they are. I don't think it'll take them long to find Celeste. Unless we get them first."

They opened the French windows to let in the cool night air. They set out the food on a table next to the window, and for the first time in several days Espinosa put some music on. Slowly, as the wine registered in their bodies, they started taking off their clothes. Irene hugged Espinosa tight, first on the chair in the living room, then on the floor, and if they had had more outdoor space than a two-foot-wide balcony, they would have made love in the open air. Since they didn't, they moved to the bed.

It was eight o'clock. The sun was up and Irene had left the table set for breakfast. He'd never figured out how she could rise so early in the morning, get ready, prepare breakfast, and leave, all without ever making the slightest sound. He preferred to attribute it to Irene's discretion rather than the effects of the wine. He showered, imagining Irene still there with him—preferably also in the shower.

Before nine, it was already hot. He walked on the shaded side of the street on the way to the station. He saw no sign that he was under surveillance. Most of the cars around his building were the same as always, and the ones that weren't were empty. If someone was following him, he was a master. Espinosa didn't want to leave the house with Irene's clothes. He'd do that only under conditions of absolute security. As soon as he got to the station, he advised the group to keep lunch open, and told one of them to come by a half hour before to learn where.

They went to the same Italian place they'd gone to the last time. It wasn't far, and he'd known the owner for so long that he could trust him; even so, they sat at a different table. They discussed the case before ordering their food, which forced even the wordiest among them to hone their synthesizing skills. Espinosa opened the meeting.

"We haven't learned anything in the last five days. If any progress has been made, it's been entirely on the killer's side. We already know that the death in Leme wasn't a suicide, that the victim wasn't Celeste, and that the killer threw the wrong woman out of the window. That means that the profile of Celeste is imperfect or out of date: he knew where she was, but he didn't have a recent photo, which made him confuse the two women, both of whom were former strippers, same age, with similar faces and body types. I'm not surprised he had the basic information right: whoever gave him the information about the cops he killed also provided descriptions of the mistresses. What I don't understand is how he tracked down Celeste's friend's address."

"He could have gotten it the same way Welber and Artur got it," said Ramiro.

"It's possible. But if he'd done that, he would have also gotten information about Rosita, and he wouldn't have confused her with the other woman. If he got it wrong, it's because he didn't even know they looked alike. He only had the address."

"It's tough to think a guy as good as he is would have botched something so simple."

"That's what I'm trying to say. He didn't get it wrong, he

just didn't know what she looked like, and the proof that he's good is that he talked to Rosita before killing her. The purpose of the discussion was to confirm her identity."

"So why did he kill her?"

"Because when he saw the purse, which obviously had her ID in it, she got there faster, grabbed it, and threw it out the window. He took the action as proof that it was Celeste. Rosita saved her friend and lost her life."

"It makes sense," said Ramiro.

"What I still don't understand is how he got her address," Espinosa continued. "It's possible that you're being followed, though that wouldn't mean the murderer would know in advance where you're going. In any case, be aware of the possibility. Welber, I want you to go to Celeste's apartment and see if anything is missing, particularly any photographs. Do it as soon as we're finished here."

The discussion thereafter was purely tactical. No progress had been made in terms of identifying the murderer.

"If nobody has anything further, we can order our food."

At the sight of food, the group's spirits rose. It occurred to Espinosa that it would be nice if he could do this sort of thing more often, take other cops out for lunch. Then again, he didn't relish the thought of quality time with most of his colleagues. The group left the restaurant in pairs, Ramiro with Artur and Espinosa with Welber.

"Chief, I've got good news for you."

"I need some good news."

"They opened a used-book store only a block from the station."

The news had an effect Welber hadn't expected. The chief stopped walking, stared as if he hadn't heard, and started walking again.

"You didn't like the news, sir?"

"I did. Thanks, Welber."

"Did something happen that I didn't notice, sir?"

"No, Welber. Sorry. You gave me a great piece of news, but it reminds me of something else . . ."

"Something unpleasant?"

"No, something pleasant, as long as it remains a fantasy, but when it becomes real it's a bit of a shock."

"But you've always liked books and bookstores."

"True. So much that I've always thought I could dedicate my life to them. It's when I see someone else doing just that, so close by, that I get scared. In any case, it's great news. Thanks."

At the end of the afternoon, on his way back home, he took his usual route. He didn't think he'd been ready to hear about the bookstore. Maybe he'd stop by the next day. Maybe Saturday, when he had more time. Besides, he didn't need any new reading material. He'd barely started the Woolrich book he'd inherited from his grandmother.

The meeting with the chief was one of those telling little incidents that kept Serena from being like other respectable ladies. In her eyes, a real lady was beautiful, elegant, imperturbable. Serena, however, liked to stir the pot, to do things proper ladies might want to do but wouldn't dare, either out of cowardice or ignorance. Her meeting with the policeman gave her the pleasantly intense, though vague feeling that she'd done something thrillingly illicit.

But at the end of the day, she had witnessed a murder, and that was why she had been in contact with the officer. She had to be careful not to let anything diminish the importance of that fact. She knew that she hadn't called the police out of a desire to be a good citizen but because there was something else, something deeper, that connected her to that woman. She didn't feel connected to her in the way that two different people can feel a bond; she felt like they were two parts of the same person. She had never tried to learn what the woman's name was, but it didn't matter. She could give the woman her own name. Not her last name, which had only been tacked on her later, but her name alone: Serena.

None of this affected Guilherme. The death of the woman was simply a topic for morbid curiosity, and he didn't think about it for more than a minute, even though she had been crushed on the sidewalk only a few feet from his building. Guilherme was interested in only two things, neither of which required much imagination: economics and golf. And the second interested him only because it was so tightly connected with the first.

That afternoon, at five, there was a meeting in the Largo do Machado. It was only ten past two. She knew from experience that nothing could satisfactorily fill that time. There was nothing to do but wait.

She arrived forty minutes early, parked in an underground garage, studied the windows of the two bookstores on the way to the building where the meeting would be held. When she reached the room, at a little before five, there were about ten people there already, half of whom were busy setting up the chairs. It was a testimonial meeting, and the first to speak was a woman. The stories were all variations on the same theme, which didn't necessarily make them monotonous. Every one was a distinct event, with its own intensity and its own personal effect. Serena had already heard hundreds of similar stories, but to her they were like jazz: the players sounded the same theme, yet their interpretations were original and unique. She didn't stay until the end. For some of the people there that afternoon, talking was more important than the duration of their abstinence.

After lunch, instead of going back to the station with the rest of the group, Espinosa headed home, placed Irene's clothes in a bag, and got in his car, parked almost directly in front of his building. Since he'd been transferred from the Praça Mauá downtown to Copacabana, he rarely used his car. If he couldn't walk, he took the subway or a cab. Sometimes his car stayed in the same spot for more than a week at a time, which led to mechanical and electrical problems, meaning that he often couldn't use the car when he needed it most. Yet another reason not to use it.

But that afternoon the engine started up on the third try. Espinosa left the Peixoto District by the Rua Anita Garibaldi, carefully checking the rearview mirror. He drove around for a few blocks until he was sure nobody was following him, then stopped two blocks away from his starting point, at the entrance to a dry cleaners. He asked them to iron the clothes, gave the address of the Hotel Santa Clara, and instructed the delivery to be made to Miss Ângela Cardoso. He then returned to the Peixoto District, parked his car in the same spot, and proceeded on foot to the station.

While he was walking, he thought about the fact that he was simultaneously preoccupied with three women. Not with the same intensity, not with the same affection, but they all had their place in his mind. With daylight savings time, it was five after three, but it was really five after two on a hot, breezeless summer day. He walked slowly, keeping to the shadows, in an almost useless attempt to arrive at work relatively sweat-free. Since he was still only halfway there, he thought about taking off his jacket, which, though it was light and made of linen, was still a jacket.

But doing that would require removing his gun from his belt and hiding it from passersby. The operation required two steps. Without breaking his stride, he unclipped his weapon from his belt and moved it to his pants pocket, where it protruded as obviously as if he were holding it in his hand. The second step was to remove his coat and drape it over his arm, which helped conceal the bulge in his pants. When he was done, he was sweating even more profusely than before.

Serena had been in her dressing room for more than two hours with the light turned off, watching the apartment across the street. She'd taken the adjustable chair from the office and extended it as high as it could go. Even without sitting directly at the window, she had an ample view of the other building. The dead woman's apartment was still dark. Most of the others reflected the blue light of the television screen, all tuned to the first evening soap opera. She tried one more time to use the binoculars she'd brought from the living room, but they were too powerful for the short distance. All she saw when she tried to focus was a big dark something with unusual reflections. It took her a while to realize that it was the glass of the living room window. When she focused on the apartments below, she could make out the details of objects resting on the furniture.

She turned her attention back to the empty apartment. She had the clear impression that it wasn't, in fact, entirely empty. This wasn't a hallucination or an illusion: she wasn't seeing furniture where nothing was there; there were no paintings on the walls or people walking through the rooms. Everything was as dark and empty as ever, but she could have sworn that someone was there, in the darkest corner of the room, looking at her. It was as if the other person's gaze gave off light. Her window was closed, which would make it impossible for someone across the way to see her. Even though she knew this, she was scared. Her hands and armpits were damp, something that rarely happened to her. She had been sitting still for a long time when she heard her husband arrive. Before he could turn on the light in the adjacent room, exposing her lookout, she got up to meet him.

"Hi, honey, were you in the dark? I'm sorry I'm so late; we had a last-minute meeting."

"No problem. We didn't have any plans."

"Did you eat?"

"I was waiting for you to come home."

"Do you want to go out or eat in?"

"We have plenty here."

"Any news from the officer?"

"No. And I don't think there will be any, either. I just reported something. What he does with it is up to him. I don't have anything else to do with it."

"I hope you're right."

"You were really impressed that I spoke to a police chief."

"You didn't speak to him; you had lunch with him in the restaurant next to our house."

"We didn't have lunch, just an orange juice."

"Wouldn't have made much difference to people who saw you together."

"Fuck, Guilherme, you're making it sound like I went to a motel with him."

"That's how he might see it."

"No! No, he won't! The only one who thinks that is you!"

"Let's agree that you have a certain thing for the underworld."

"Which is more interesting than the overworld where you live."

"Not where *I* live, where *we* live."

"If you call that a life . . ."

It could have gone on for hours. In fact, it had been going on for years. Serena thought it was best to go take care of dinner while Guilherme showered and changed. When they sat down at the table, they had calmed down.

"Please, let's not fight during dinner," Guilherme said.

Serena answered, "I'm not fighting with you, just saying what I think. How was the meeting?"

"Fine. But as a result I have to go to Washington this week."

"Ha, ha."

"That's it? Ha, ha?"

"Baby, it's your world and your job. Washington is less newsworthy than São Paulo for you."

"It's not the trip, it's what I have to do there."

"I'm sure that you'll do great, whatever it is."

"You used to be more interested in my work."

"And you used to be more interested in me."

Before going to bed, Serena sat for a few more minutes in the dressing room, looking across at the other building.

Ramiro lived in Grajaú, in the Zona Norte. He wasn't sure if getting transferred to Copacabana had been a reward, as his superiors had said, or a punishment. To get from his house to Copacabana he had to catch a bus to the Praça Saens Pena, in Tijuca, and take the subway from there to Copacabana. If he wanted to get there at the same time as his boss, he had to leave home an hour earlier. That morning, they arrived simultaneously.

"Morning, boss."

"Morning, Ramiro. Anything new?"

"I'd like you to call the group together."

"Fine. Tell Artur and Welber."

Since the group had been established, the chief had been treated very differently. Even the people who used to be on close terms with Espinosa, out of friendship or long acquaintance, had started speaking to him more formally. Any chatting in the hallways or on the stairs ceased immediately when Espinosa appeared; in an effort not to draw attention to their special relationship with the boss, Ramiro, Artur, and Welber made a point of addressing him as officially as possible, which sometimes sounded a little phony. This wasn't the work environment Espinosa had meant to instill when he'd been transferred from the Praça Mauá, and it didn't suit his personality. But he knew that when people started killing cops and other cops were suspected, the least you could expect was a chillier workplace climate.

A little after eleven-thirty, Ramiro came into Espinosa's office, followed by Welber and Artur. They arranged to meet an hour later, in the same restaurant. From the outset, they had agreed that any member of the group could convene a meeting. As an inspector and the head of the detectives, Ramiro would normally call in Welber and Artur for a meeting without informing, let alone asking permission from the chief. But this was a special group, and for safety's sake everyone needed to know what the others were doing.

Because Ramiro had called the meeting, he began speaking once everyone had sat down and poured themselves some water.

"I have a few ideas. Nothing more than a hunch and a few inconsistent clues, but it might be a beginning. Here goes. I began with the chief's idea, that nobody was killing the cops for personal revenge. I agree. So why? To punish them, perhaps. The guys were guilty of something, so someone hired a killer. Then the problem became: what were they guilty of? Answer: fucking up. They were punished because they made a mistake. A big mistake. They fucked up something they couldn't afford to. Now, everyone makes mistakes. In our business, I think we get more stuff wrong than right, actually. If every cop who made a mistake was killed, the police force would have disappeared a long time ago. So these guys screwed up something that they absolutely couldn't afford to screw up. They must have committed a mortal sin. And I thought, what is a cop's mortal sin? Answer: betrayal. Maybe these guys had betrayed their partners. But what partners, damn it? We're their partners, we're all in the police, but nobody had felt betrayed by any of them. There was another problem: what kind of betrayal? It could only be theft or snitching. So I started looking with that in mind. I know where our colleagues hang out. I started to dig around, hearing rumors, inserting myself into conversations and listening more than talking. Lots of them know me and know I work in the Twelfth Precinct with Officer Espinosa. They know we're investigating these murders, so they clammed up. They want to know why their colleagues are being killed; they're afraid, and they want to get the killer, too. Some of them opened up, though, just a little. It was like hide-and-seek. I've been doing this for a few days, and I think I've managed to come up with a couple of things."

"Material proof?" Welber asked.

"No. Suppositions. Nothing proven. Little bits here and there."

"And what did you get?"

"The illegal 'animal' lottery. The three cops collected and distributed the lottery mob's contribution to the police. They weren't the only ones involved. Apparently, they've been doing it for years. They were the middlemen, so there was no way to make sure they were distributing everything they got from the gangsters, but not even the lottery mob or the cops thought anyone would be stupid enough to try to cheat both of them. Rumor has it that when someone found out they'd been cheated, they decided to rub them out."

"Who decided? The police or the mob?" Espinosa asked.

"That I couldn't find out."

"How much credibility do you give these stories?"

"Chief, I believe it. Not everything was given to me so cleanly, but here and there I started putting the pieces together."

"And why did they kill the women?"

"Because the cops divided up the money in their apartments here in the Zona Sul, and the mistresses were sometimes around. They must have been scared that the mistresses would say something."

"Were those three the only ones?"

"I don't know, but I didn't hear about any others."

"What doesn't make sense to me," Espinosa said, "is that they killed the women as well. If it was a punishment, why were they killed? The men were stealing, not the women; they didn't participate actively. At most they could have been seen as passive accomplices."

"And what if they knew the names of the people who got money and decided to talk, for revenge?"

"Do you think Celeste knows the name of the people who were on the take?"

"It's possible, Chief."

During the rest of the afternoon, Espinosa thought about Ramiro's speculations. On his way home, at the end of the day, he was still pondering them. If the detective was right, the series of cop killings might have reached its end, since the murderer had started focusing on the women. The reasonable supposition would be that the murderer had taken care of the cops first, before turning to the mistresses. The men were the main target, not the women. If this was true, the killer still had to eliminate Celeste.

The light on the answering machine was blinking in the dark living room. He turned on a lamp, opened the windows to let out the hot afternoon air, and pressed the button to listen to the messages. The first was from the bank, telling him that his car insurance was about to expire and informing him that a simple phone call would be enough to renew it automatically. The second was from Irene, asking if the clothes had worked for the woman. The third was from Celeste: "Espinosa, the presents you sent me will be perfect in my new house. Talk to you later. Ângela."

He ran down the stairs, trying to remember where the closest pay phone was. He crossed the street in the direction of the square and found not one but two phones. He dialed Celeste's hotel.

"Hotel Santa Clara, good evening."

"I'd like to speak with Ângela Cardoso, please. I don't know the room number."

"She left the hotel this afternoon, sir."

"How? She just left? Alone or with someone else?"

"The hotel doesn't give out that kind of information."

"I'm Chief Espinosa from the Twelfth Precinct, and I need to know."

"She left by herself, sir."

"Thank you."

He went back to his apartment and listened to the message again in the hope of discovering some hidden insinuation, but there was nothing. It wasn't the text of the message that was opaque, but the reason why she would abandon a seemingly safe hiding place.

PART 3

1

He left his house later than usual. He wanted to stop by the used-book store Welber had told him about, but he figured it wouldn't be open until nine. It was en route to the station, but Espinosa rarely passed that way. As Welber had said, it was about halfway down the block. He wasn't planning on going in. He preferred to circle around it gradually, allowing himself time to get used to the idea. For a long time, he'd dreamed about the day he could quit the police force and open a bookstore. That was his secret reason for hanging on to all the books he'd inherited from his grandmother. They were kept in boxes piled floor to ceiling in his unused maid's room. Together with his own collection, they were his initial capital. Actual capital he could get with his police pension. It wasn't quite a plan; it was more of an idea. He'd fantasized about owning a bookstore since he was a law student hanging out in the bookstores around the Largo São Francisco, downtown. Now, according to Welber, this fantasy had been invaded by real people who had materialized a few steps from the station. A used-book store in Copacabana, halfway between his house and the station, was something he couldn't have ever imagined.

At the corner, he was already scouting it out. It didn't

take him long to spot the little shelves outside with the sale books. He slowed down and gazed at the window. He glanced inside and continued on to the station. It was Thursday. Maybe Saturday afternoon . . .

2

Officer Espinosa had given her not only his number at work but his number at home. Serena didn't know if that was a sign of his professional competence or if it was meant to suggest that he was open to more personal communication. This latter possibility was hinted at by the handwritten addendum of the number at the bottom of the standard police card. She'd looked at it dozens of times, as if expecting some hidden truth to emerge from the handwriting. She even dreamed about the officer, but that shed little light on her situation. She believed more in intuition than in facts; during their meeting, she could tell that he was interested in her. She'd seen how hard it was for him to keep his eyes off her chest. Now, stretched out in bed, she looked at the card one more time before getting up for breakfast.

Guilherme had left for work early. Things to take care of before the trip, he'd said. And she had no doubt that he was indeed taking care of professional matters; it hadn't ever occurred to her that he could be involved with some other woman. There was no woman, herself included, that could give him more pleasure than exercising political power. For someone like him, Washington was infinitely more alluring than even the hottest sexual encounter. So as long as her husband was in the administration, she knew that she had nothing to fear from other women, unless a fetching lady Cabinet secretary appeared on the scene.

She remained in bed a little longer, imagining the officer's private life. Not married. That she was sure of. She could always spot a married man, whether he wore a ring or not. Marriage was like a vaccination: it immunized and left a mark. He didn't look like he'd just lost a wife; he didn't have the friskiness of men who've recently gotten their freedom and are ready to take on any woman. Nor did he have the melancholy of those men who had lost their taste for sex. He certainly wasn't asexual: that was clear enough from the way he'd been looking at her. Maybe he was most given to occasional, quick, risk-free relationships.

Over breakfast, she thought about her husband's trip. He traveled so much that she didn't even really notice it anymore. But this trip seemed like a happy coincidence. She didn't need her husband to be in Washington to do what she wanted, but with him out of the way her time was much freer. It wasn't that she didn't like him; their lives were comfortable, and anything dull or uninteresting could easily be overcome with a bit of imagination and daring.

She'd met the cop on Monday. Now it was Thursday. It was time to get back in touch. There were two numbers printed on the card: one general, for the station; and a direct line. She used the direct line.

"Dona Serena, what a pleasure to hear your voice."

"Same to you, Officer. I don't want to meddle with your work, but I can't get the death of that girl out of my head . . ."

For Espinosa, Serena was an unknown quantity. In her first appearance, downtown, she'd seemed seductive and unapproachable. She'd looked as if she'd just met a lover. In her second incarnation, she'd been friendly and helpful. Now, on the phone, she still seemed friendly but was a little more enigmatic. As charming as she was, though, Espinosa was focused on protecting Celeste. The girl had gotten the clothes—he understood that from the message she'd left on the answering machine—but something had scared her into abandoning her hiding place. He didn't think it was likely that the murderer had made it through all the hotels in the Zona Sul so quickly, discovering a woman when he didn't even seem to know what she looked like. Or Celeste was more clever than he'd thought and was continuously on the move, changing her name and appearance. The house she'd referred to on the message was clearly a new hiding place. Now he had to see if she'd get in touch to tell him where she was.

At the end of the morning, Welber came into the office to report on his visit to Celeste's apartment.

"Chief, it doesn't look like they've taken any pictures."

"Are you sure?"

"There are pictures in all the frames, and there's no sign that anyone has broken in."

"Who was there last?"

"I think it was Ramiro."

"Did you ask the doormen?"

"I did. They said nobody else had been there."

The individual updates were still delivered in the chief's office. Only the group meetings were held outside the station, though everyone was beginning to doubt how useful that measure was. Official meetings were meant to be held on the premises; little meetings outside the station gave other policemen the impression that they were being excluded from some important discussion—which, in fact, they were. On Friday morning, Welber told the boss what he'd learned.

"Sir, it's almost impossible to report everyone who's on the take. They just think it's part of their pay. They look at bribes like a legitimate bonus that can double their salary, or more. The problem isn't identifying everyone who's on the take. Everyone knows, because so many people are involved, after all. The problem is getting anyone to talk, especially because they know we're investigating. You yourself know who's corrupt. But so what? What are you going to do? Fire everyone?"

"We're not investigating corruption. That's something for the attorney general's office. We're looking into who killed three cops and their lovers and why they were killed."

"Exactly. According to Ramiro, the guys were killed because they were dipping into the money that was supposed to be distributed. It was almost like they'd stolen their colleagues' salaries."

"But their colleagues are precisely the people who want

to find out who the killer is. Remember what Nestor said to me on the street."

"Until they found out why the murders happened. As soon as that happened, nobody was interested in investigating anything. I think that as soon as they heard that there was no serial killer bumping off cops, as soon as they found out it was a punishment, they calmed down. They didn't want to keep investigating. They didn't want anything to come between them and their tips."

"Did you learn anything about Celeste's whereabouts?"

"She vanished completely. We checked the morgue, the hospitals, the airports, and we spent a long time at the bus station—at this time of the year almost five thousand people a day go through there, and it's almost impossible to find anyone. Either she's managed to get out of town and is already far away, or she's found a good hiding place and isn't coming out."

"Let's go to the bar on the corner and get some coffee."

"We have coffee . . ."

"The coffee at that place is special."

On the street, the chief gripped Welber's arm to keep him from walking too fast; the bar was very close.

"Welber, I want you to hand your stuff over to Artur, and I want Ramiro to carry on with what he's doing. For the next few days, you are going to follow someone wherever they go. It has to be a pro job. Wear different clothes, try to come up with some disguise, and—most of all—be very careful. The days will be exhausting, there will be no fixed schedule, and you won't be able to count on backup. Above all else, nobody—nobody—can know what you're doing."

"Fine. Who am I supposed to follow?"

"Me."

"Huh?"

"You have to see if anyone's following me. If I try to figure it out myself, the guy's going to notice. It has to be a third person. Whoever's following me is going to be focusing on me. They won't imagine that they themselves are being followed. I don't know who's following me or if I'm even actually being followed. It could be a man or a woman. If you manage to identify anyone, stop trailing me immediately and switch over to the other person. At that point you'll have to be extra careful."

"When do I start?"

"Today, when I go home. Hold on to this. It's a prepaid cell phone, and there's no way to trace it. I've got another one with me. Take down the number and get in touch with me that way. When I'm at the station, there's no need for you to do anything. If I have to leave, I'll find a way to let you know. Same when I go home at the end of the day. I usually leave my house at the same time. I'll let you come up with a more detailed strategy. Pay close attention to one thing: if I can see you, my stalker can see you too. You'll have to be invisible for both of us."

3

Espinosa didn't notice anyone when he left that night or when he went home, neither Welber nor anybody else who may have been on his tail. While he was getting ready for bed, he heard a noise that was neither the phone nor the alarm clock. The cell phone! He couldn't remember where he'd put it. On the living room table.

"Hello."

"Chief?"

"Sorry, Welber, I'm still not used to this thing. And sorry that I didn't tell you I was going out . . ."

"No problem, sir. Nobody except me was following you today. It was tough to watch you eat that pasta and wine."

"Welber, you've done great. I could have sworn that nobody was following me."

"Afterward you can get me my medal. What we need to figure out now is this: I'm doing this by myself, so I need to sleep when you're asleep. There's nobody to take my place at night."

"Right. When I go home at night, call and tell me that you're going home. I'd suggest that you stay in that little hotel here for the next couple of days. It'll make things easier."

"That's where I'm calling from, sir."

Since it was impossible to take care all of his pending domestic tasks that Saturday morning, he started off with the most important things first: coffee and newspapers. The phone rang around noon. Irene.

"Hey, honey, I was just calling to see if there was any news of the girl."

"She vanished."

"Vanished? But didn't you know where she was?"

"I did, but for some reason she abandoned her hiding place and disappeared."

"You think the murderer . . ."

"No. She called me to thank me for the clothes and said she was moving, but she didn't say why."

"Does that get in the way of our little dinner plans?"

"I'd love to see you, but I don't think it's such a good idea."

"Why?"

"If I'm being followed, I don't want them to see us together. They might want to use you."

"Are you being followed?"

"I think so, and I don't have any good way to protect you."

"From who?"

"The guy who's stalking the girl."

"And what could he do to me?"

"Make a trade."

"Huh?"

"He wants Celeste. He could get you and try to trade her for you."

"You mean kidnap me?"

"Right."

"So as long as this thing lasts, we won't be able to see each other?"

"It's not going to last long."

"You didn't answer me."

"I don't want to expose you."

"Espinosa, we're not going to fuck in the middle of the street."

"That's hardly necessary. All they need to know is that I like you."

"And do you?"

"I like you."

"Jesus, it only takes a half dozen murders and a kidnapping to get you to say that!"

"You already knew that."

"Yeah, but you're supposed to say it!"

"All right. I like you."

"I like you too."

"And now? Can we spend the night together?"

"Call me before you leave and come in a cab. I'll wait for you at the entrance to the building. If you don't see me, don't get out, and go straight home."

"*Jawohl, mein Kommandant.*"

"Huh?"

"My German classes. See you."

Irene's phone call had come just as he was getting ready to deal with the toaster. It wasn't serious. The machine was still toasting one side of each slice, and both slots were still working. It would have been worse if he could toast only one piece at a time, one side at a time. He didn't think it was unreasonable to put off fixing it until the following Saturday.

He had lunch close to home, without paying too much attention to what he was eating, and then headed over to the bookstore. This time, he had steeled himself for a good look. When he got there, he found a sign posted inside the door: "Open at 2:00 P.M." His watch read one-twenty. He looked at the sale books in the window, tried to make out the inside of the dark store, and went back home.

When Irene called later that evening to let him know that she was on her way, the sky was cloudless and the night was starry. He waited five minutes before going down. He didn't want to stand inside the door, because she wouldn't see him; he propped open the door and went outside, standing under the tiny awning that sheltered a little colonial-style lamp. The light from the building lit him from behind, and the lamp lit him from above. For someone who felt that he was being followed and watched, he thought that the only thing missing was a sign around his neck with his name written in fluorescent ink. But he didn't think it would take Irene more than fifteen minutes.

He was already feeling stupid about having agreed to see her when a taxi turned the corner and stopped in front of the building. Before opening the door to let her out, Espinosa looked around to make sure nobody had managed to sneak into the building.

After a few minutes, when the two were safely inside his apartment, the phone rang.

"Chief, after watching you stand like a stuffed dummy for fifteen minutes, and after seeing Dona Irene arrive, I thought I could go to sleep."

"If I'd known that you were there, I wouldn't have worried so much. Of course you can go to sleep. Good night."

"Good night, sir."

"Who was that?" Irene asked while she was arranging the things she'd brought on the table.

"Welber, my temporary guardian angel."

"Are you in danger?"

"Not really, but I'm being watched. They're not interested in me, but in the woman you loaned the clothes to. I think they're following me to get to her."

"And can they?"

"Only if she comes looking for me."

"And is that what's worrying you?"

"Not too much."

"But there's something on your mind, or you wouldn't be twitching like that."

"They opened a used-book store a couple of blocks away."

"Great! What's the problem?"

"That was what I was going to do if I ever left the police."

"Sell used books?"

"Why not?"

"Because you're not a businessman. You don't understand the book market, you don't have the money to start a business, you don't know how much rent on a shop is here in Copacabana . . ."

"You've just liquidated my dream of someday leaving the police force to open a bookstore."

"You're a romantic."

"Is that so bad?"

"No, it's marvelous . . . for love, not for business."

"So let's open the wine."

4

She didn't have to do anything besides sign a temporary rent contract; the owner hadn't made any unusual demands. Since it was the end of the summer holidays, the real estate agency hadn't had an easy time finding someone interested. And there was the little matter of the defenestration of the last resident. All Serena had to do was pay the first month's rent in advance.

The doorman immediately recognized the woman from the neighboring building who had previously been asking questions about the apartment.

"You're not going to trade in that great apartment for this one, are you, ma'am?"

"I'm writing a book and I need somewhere isolated and close to home, and this is perfect. All I have to do is cross the street."

"I don't think the doctor left much in the apartment. You can look yourself."

The conversation between the two filled the time it took the elevator to arrive at the tenth floor.

"The doctor asked me to tell you how the gas heater works and how to turn on the light switches. Let's open the windows to get rid of the paint smell. The rest is all there. The kitchen has a microwave. If you need anything, just call down."

"What's your name?"

"It's Josualdo, ma'am, but everyone calls me Aldo."

"Thank you, Josualdo."

"Aldo's fine, ma'am, you can call me Aldo."

"Okay, Aldo. I don't think I'm going to need anything. The only thing I'm going to bring is my computer, and it fits inside my bag."

"Did you know Dona Rosita, ma'am?"

"Only by sight."

A few trips across the street were sufficient to bring the things she needed for her stay in the apartment. The phone line hadn't been disconnected, which was good. At the end of the afternoon she had set up everything in the bathroom and the kitchen. She'd put a few changes of clothes in the wardrobe and placed her computer on top of the only table in the living room. The apartment would have been nice if all the furniture hadn't been thrown in there without any coherent decorating scheme. One thing, though, was great: the side view toward the beach. From the wide window you could glimpse a stretch of sea that, even though it was narrow, lent the apartment a certain amplitude. In comparison, the view from her own room was like looking at the sea through a keyhole.

Serena didn't know what to do. The truth was, she didn't have anything planned. All she could do was wait for something. She didn't know what and she didn't know when. From her new window, she sat looking at the building across the street, looking at her other window. Rosita had probably seen her in her dressing room, trying on a dress for some dinner party. She had the almost crazy feeling that she was about to see herself appear naked in the other window, fresh from the shower.

Guilherme would not be getting back from Washington until the end of the week, which meant that her next five days were completely free. She wouldn't stop going to her meetings, and she wouldn't stop going to the shrink, even though she was no longer interested in her analysis. She had nothing else scheduled.

She sat watching the ocean change from light green to deep green until it grew completely dark. Every day she would sit at the window for a while, something she rarely did in her own apartment, where the living room view took in all of Copacabana Beach. In her new window, the important thing was not to see but to be seen.

A few steps from the station was A Polaca Restaurant. The food was good, but it was too close; a little farther was the Italian place, which he preferred to save for his free time, even though he'd used it for the first few meetings. There were also the many food-by-the-pound places, bakeries, places with chickens roasting in the window. There was always McDonald's, only a block away. He decided to cross the street and get a sandwich and a juice at a little diner, a meal he could eat in the air-conditioned environment of his office.

Every day it became clearer to Espinosa how insufferably predictable routine police work had become. He didn't know how much longer he would last. He only knew that it was a matter of time. Ten years or ten days: above all, he didn't want to reach the point at which every day became a kind of anesthetic, transforming pain, sadness, and suffering into a permanent tedium, a tedium present night and day, at work and at home, transforming real emotions into simple indifference. He'd often thought about leaving the police force. At first it had been over ethical matters, but recently he had come to believe that it was the routine that was killing him. Even a decade ago he'd been more interested in the stakeouts and the night shifts, but those activities were reserved for younger men, like Welber and Artur. All he had to do was begin and end investigations and push his pen. He had become an armed desk.

At the end of the afternoon, Ramiro arrived to give his report.

"May I, sir?"

"Come in, Ramiro."

"I came alone because you wanted us to do this individually."

"Right. How are things going?"

"Not great. I'm not making any progress. Nobody's helping, nobody's telling me anything. When they see me coming, they clear out. And there's no way anyone will talk to me alone. They want to be sure everyone knows they're not snitching on anybody else. I still think my hypothesis is correct, but I think we'll have to shift the focus of the investigation for a while. I've been looking so hard that I've found something that I hadn't seen before. Maybe I'll see where that leads and let the lottery people cool off for a while."

"What did you discover?"

"That they were also involved with cars. I don't know exactly how; it could just be a red herring. But I think it's worth checking out."

"Fine. Do it."

That night, at home, he got a call from Welber on the cell phone.

"Chief, can we talk?"

"Sure. How are you? I still haven't seen you."

"Great, you're not supposed to."

"Did you manage to find anyone?"

"Yesterday afternoon I thought so, but I have my doubts. They drove around the square twice, slowing down every time they passed your building. It was Sunday, so it might have been someone looking at apartments. But they did the same thing tonight. It was dark, so I can't be sure it was the same person, but it was the same car."

"A man?"

"A woman."

"Look familiar?"

"No. I thought it might be Celeste, but I can't be sure. I don't even know if the person's really looking for you, but I'm on the case."

"Did you get the license number?"

"I did. I asked the transportation department to run it, and they'll give me an answer in the morning."

"Are you managing to rest?"

"Of course, sir. You lead a quiet life."

5

Serena got to the afternoon meeting a half hour early. Dora was the only one in the room when she arrived, her broken leg stretched out onto the chair in front of her, smoking a cigarette. Her third, Serena guessed from the two butts in the ashtray on her lap. Serena tapped the plaster cast lightly, as if to wake up the broken leg, and Dora patted her head in return. Almost everyone who made their way into the room knew everybody else. With time and practice, Serena had learned to distinguish the different kinds of stories. She knew that the people who spoke most elegantly, in formal, well-constructed narratives, who used the right words in the right places, were the people who had separated themselves the most from their stories. Others, who spoke hesitantly, whose stories were as much about the gaps as about the words, who started and stopped, who seemed still shocked by what had happened to them, were the people who had still not exorcised the horror. Their testimonials were not necessarily truer than the others, but Serena thought their truth was of a different order. Whenever the meeting's leader asked her to share her story, she tried to focus on the most immediate experiences, those most vivid in her mind. Today, the first person told a long, intense, truthful story, one that touched her deeply. As usual, Serena was seated close to the door; she left before the second person began speaking.

At home, she waited for Guilherme to call. The calls always took place at the same time, and their content never varied. As the years had gone by, those calls had been reduced to electric impulses, devoid of excess content, including affection. For some reason she didn't understand, they had kept up the habit. She ate a salad and some grilled fish, pulled on shorts and a T-shirt, and headed out to her new, temporary apartment. The doorman was still eyeing the new tenant with mistrust.

"Evening, ma'am. Is everything all set up now?"

"There wasn't much to do."

"You know, ma'am, if you need anything, just give me a call."

"Thanks."

For the second time, the same doorman had made the same offer. The way he did it, the tone of his voice, the look in his eye were all perfectly professional, but she thought there was something more to it. The elevator wasn't quick and quiet like the one in her building; the open door allowed the noise of the machine to be heard throughout the building as it banged its way upward. But it arrived efficiently at the tenth floor.

She entered the apartment without turning on the light. She wanted to recapture the feeling she'd had a couple of days after the woman's murder, when she'd looked into this apartment and had the definite feeling that someone in the darkness was looking back at her.

Two other windows in her own apartment faced this way: the one in the bedroom and the one in Guilherme's study. The same was true of the apartments on the other floors. Surveying the position of the windows—some were farther away, some were on lower floors—Serena realized that she had a good view of what went on in four apartments: twelve windows in all.

She was most struck by the contrast between the movement in the other apartments and the inert darkness of her own. She quickly tired of looking into the other apartments and concentrated on her own window. While she was looking, she kept the light off in her new perch. Even though she knew it was her apartment and her window, there was a new mystery to the darkness, as if something were about to happen. She sat on the sill for a while. She couldn't see a thing. She knew where the furniture was, but she couldn't make it out. She shielded her eyes from the light from the street-lamps and the other apartments, making little binoculars with her hands. She secretly expected to see the shadowy assassin in the dark corners of her apartment. She moved away from the window and turned on the light. The room she was in was not a neutral environment. Even with the light on, she was in more danger there than in the room across the street. In this same room, a woman more or less her age, perhaps with a similar past, had fought with someone who'd become, a couple of minutes later, her murderer. Before she'd died, she had thrown her purse out of the window. Whatever the reason behind that action, it had cost her her life.

Serena thought about calling the officer, but she didn't

have a reason to, unless she cut straight to the point. She opened her Filofax and found his card. At that hour, she'd have to call him at home, rather than the station. She dialed the number he'd written by hand. Before anyone answered, she hung up. She closed the window, turned off the light, and left. She crossed the street and entered her building. But instead of going up, she went into the garage, got her car, and headed for the Peixoto District.

What does a single policeman do at night? She didn't know if he was by himself. She would have liked him to be. He surely wasn't watching TV; the light in his window was yellow, not blue. Maybe he was reading or listening to music. Did policeman read and listen to music? It was a little after nine. He could have been in the bedroom instead of the living room. She drove around the square one more time but didn't wait to see if there was any change in his apartment. She headed back to Leme.

An hour after Espinosa arrived at work on Tuesday morning, Welber came into his office with a piece of paper.

"It's a copy of the car's registration. The address is written on the back."

The car's owner was Guilherme Afonso Rodes, and the address was Serena Rodes's. Espinosa was completely taken aback. What was Serena doing driving around the square and checking out his apartment? Why hadn't she called instead? He wanted to pick up the phone then and there, but that would clue her in to the fact that someone was guarding him. He preferred to see what Mrs. Guilherme Afonso Rodes would do next.

"What computer did this come in on?"

"I got it myself from the transportation department."

"Great."

"What do you think?"

"This doesn't fit. She doesn't have anything to do with the reasons I told you to follow me."

"But she was after you, I'm sure of it."

"But it doesn't make sense."

"Have you known her long?"

"We only met once. I mean, twice, but the first time she didn't see me."

"What do you mean?"

"I saw her once before, at a bar downtown, but she didn't notice me. It was the afternoon you called to tell me they'd killed Silveira. It could only be a coincidence."

"Sir, I don't want to get personal, but she may be interested in you. There's no need for a reason. It happens all the time."

"She's married."

"And?"

"And what?"

"She could be interested in you, Chief."

Espinosa didn't know what to think. Obviously, nothing before the initial call could justify any personal interest. She could have gotten interested only after the meeting in Leme. There was still the question of the first encounter, downtown, but she didn't seem to have registered that.

A little after ten, the switchboard passed through a call.

"Officer Espinosa?"

"Yes."

"I have a message for you from Celeste Cardoso. She's moved but told me to tell you that she'll be in touch as soon as possible."

"Who is this? Hello? Hello?"

Before the end of the morning, there was another call.

"Officer Espinosa?"

"Yes, go ahead!"

"Is something going on?"

"Dona Serena, sorry. How are you?"

"Sir, would you have an hour free before the end of the day, around five?"

"If nothing comes up before then, I think I do."

"Then let's hope nothing does. Can we meet at the Largo do Machado, in front of the Cinema Condor, at five?"

"Sure. If I don't get there until five after, it's because something happened."

"Nothing's going to happen, sir. See you there."

"See you there, Dona Serena."

"One more thing, sir."

"Yes?"

"When we meet, we can get rid of the 'sir' and 'dona,' all right?"

"All right."

A lot happened before the end of the afternoon, but nothing serious. At five on the dot Espinosa left the Largo do Machado subway stop, right in front of the place they'd arranged to meet. He immediately spotted the figure that had attracted him a month and a half earlier. Espinosa returned her wave and reflected that in a few seconds they would be meeting like two lovers going to the theater. Serena gave her arm to Espinosa as if they were old friends, but instead of heading to the movies, she led him into a hallway and onto an elevator. They got off on the next-to-last floor and headed to a room at the end of the hallway. Espinosa had no idea what was going on but thought it was better not to ask.

The spacious area gave onto the building's inner courtyard and was well lit and ventilated. Besides the chairs arranged classroom-style, there was a table where the teacher's desk would be. Next to it was a stool. Against the wall was a small table with coffee and water. Serena and Espinosa sat close to the door. Every time the elevator stopped on their floor, someone else got off. It wasn't the busiest session, so when the meeting started the room was still two-thirds empty.

Until then, Serena hadn't explained why they were there or what was going on, although the AA decal next to the door hinted at the room's purpose. That didn't lessen Espinosa's surprise; it only heightened his curiosity. Espinosa's first supposition was that Serena was a member of that organization. There couldn't be any other reason why they were there instead of watching a movie or having a beer in one of the bars around the square.

The coordinator opened the meeting by taking his seat

at the table at the front of the room and reviewing the ob-
jectives of AA. Then he invited one of the members to
come up to the stool next to him and tell her story. Serena,
who still hadn't loosened her grip on Espinosa's arm, whis-
pered into his ear:

"Now you know. I like to cut to the chase."

"That you have," Espinosa answered.

They didn't stay until the end of the meeting. Serena
said it would go on for two hours and that she wasn't planning on speaking that day. They listened to the first three
people, and Espinosa was introduced to a few members of
"the club." After an hour they left, in the pause between
two testimonials. It was six-thirty when they arrived back
at the Largo do Machado.

"How long—"

"—have I been an alcoholic?"

"I was going to ask how long you've been in AA, but it's
the same question."

"I realized I was an alcoholic almost ten years ago, but I
only started going to AA when I was twenty-seven, right
before I married Guilherme."

"Was he an alcoholic as well?"

"Nobody *was* an alcoholic. Some people have been in the
program for twenty years and still consider themselves alcoholics. They know that a single sip will unleash something in them that won't let them stop before they've
drunk the whole bottle. Guilherme's not an alcoholic, even
though he drinks almost all day long. But not quite all day

long. After I met Guilherme, I went to a meeting almost every day. We got married the next year and almost broke up before our first anniversary. But it wasn't because of my drinking; it was because of my past. People suffer most from their memories. Memory is like a little inborn parasite that grows and grows until it almost devours you. Some people have no choice but to give in. Except in my case the parasite took hold of my husband. I don't regret my life before I met Guilherme. Before that I wasn't so worried about my drinking as I was about my voice and my performances. I thought I had a good voice and sang well. I sang and drank for five years. When I met Guilherme, I'd stopped singing and was struggling to quit drinking."

It was one of the busiest times of day in the Largo do Machado. They left and headed toward Flamengo Beach, arm in arm, and all he could think of was how that arm had ended up wrapped around his.

"From what you say, though, the worst is over."

"But not completely. It's still dangerous. It's like a rabid dog that's temporarily calmed down. Someday it can still bite you."

Espinosa called a taxi, and Serena had to unglue herself from his arm to get into the cab. As soon as they were in the back seat she took it again.

"Where to?" asked the driver.

"Leme," said Serena before Espinosa could open his mouth.

During the ride they barely spoke. When the taxi

stopped in front of her building, Serena released his arm and kissed him softly on the lips before getting out of the car. "Thanks," she said, "it was a fabulous evening!"

Standing on the sidewalk, still holding the door open, she turned around.

"Next time, no Alcoholics Anonymous."

The cell phone rang while Espinosa was in the shower. It rang for the second time when he was waiting for the lasagna to defrost in the microwave. Only one person could be calling on that number.

"What's up, Welber?"

"Who's this?"

"Who are you? Who do you want to talk to?"

"To the owner of this phone."

"I'm the owner of that phone. Who are you?"

"Doesn't matter—you don't know me."

"Where's Welber?"

"Never heard of the guy."

"So what are you doing with his phone?"

"I don't know whose phone it is. I picked it up off the ground."

"So how did you call me?"

"I just hit redial."

"Where are you?"

"In the Peixoto District."

"Where in the Peixoto District?"

"On a bench in the middle of the square."

"Wait for me. I'll be there in a few seconds."

It wasn't hard to find the man. It was dinnertime and the first soap opera was on, so the square was deserted. He was still holding the phone and looking up and around, as if waiting for someone to materialize out of the thin air. Which is more or less what happened. In less than two minutes Espinosa arrived breathlessly, still tucking in his shirt, shoelaces untied. A twenty-something kid with smooth dark hair, of apparently Japanese origin, looked at him, terrified.

"I'm the owner of the phone."

"Fine. Take it. That's why I called."

"Thanks. Sorry if I was brusque with you, but I'm waiting for an important call. Did you see who dropped the phone?"

"No. It was just sitting by the curb, on the other side of the square. It might have fallen out of someone's pocket when they were getting in a car."

"Did you see any car driving off? Any confusion? Anybody fighting?"

"No, nothing. Is it something serious?"

"I hope not. What's your name?"

"Marcelo. Marcelo Ishigara."

"Thanks, Marcelo. I'm Espinosa."

He shook the kid's hand and went back to the apartment, waiting for another call. It was eight-twenty. Espinosa hadn't managed to get the lasagna out of the microwave; the three beeps must have sounded when he was talking to the kid in the square. He ate the pasta there in the kitchen, thinking about what could have happened to Welber. He might have hurried after someone, not noticing that he'd lost his phone. Or he could have dropped it on purpose, hoping that someone would do exactly what the kid had done. A way of letting him know that something had gone wrong.

Nine-thirty. More than an hour after Marcelo Ishigara's call. Sitting on the living room couch, Espinosa looked at the lights on the hills. All he could do was wait. He felt guilty for leaving the detective alone, but there was no other way. The cops who ordinarily might have helped him were under investigation. Of course, some deserved more credit—either because, like Artur, they were new to the police force and hadn't yet been exposed to the virus of corruption or because they were honest. But his trust in Artur was far from limitless; they hadn't worked together long enough for Espinosa to be a hundred percent sure. At ten-fifteen he was still thinking along these lines when his cell phone rang. He answered quickly.

"Chief, sorry, I lost my phone."

"Welber!"

"What happened, sir, is something wrong?"

"No. I have your phone."

Espinosa told him about the kid's call and the meeting in the square.

"I had to run after a car. I'm not sure, but it might have been the same woman who was here the other night. In any case, it was a woman, unless it was a man in drag."

"Welber, listen up. It might have been a woman who

164

looks like the one you saw the other night, but I don't think it's the same one."

"If for no other reason than that you dropped her off at home only a couple of hours ago. . . . Why would she come back in her car to spy on your apartment? And sir, with all due respect, maybe you'd like to tell me what's going on with Alcoholics Anonymous."

"So you saw."

"Following orders, sir."

"I didn't know you were so good."

"Sir, I'm not. You get in the subway and get off at the Largo do Machado, meet a pretty woman, and go into a building arm in arm; I'm thinking we're going to take in a movie. Instead you get in the elevator and force me to flash my badge at the elevator operator to find out what floor you got off on. Luckily I decided to get off on the top floor and look into the courtyard. And there you are, still arm in arm, at an AA meeting. It was too much."

"And the woman you followed?"

"I didn't. I was outside the car, trying to find a place with better reception for the cell phone. That's when I noticed a woman in a cab looking up at your window. I ran back to get my car, which was on the other side of the square. When I managed to get out of the square, I couldn't tell where she'd gone; I chose the wrong side."

"Welber, there's no need to follow me anymore, unless I say otherwise."

"You sure, Chief?"

"Don't worry. Celeste knows my phone might be

bugged. The one at the station is just as suspect, and the best way for her to find me is personally, without warning. Maybe she felt someone was watching her. She's really sly, and she's afraid of getting killed."

"I don't think she could have felt me watching her. Even when I was in full sight she would never have suspected me. If you yourself looked right at me, you wouldn't have recognized me. Should I quit now?"

"Go home and rest; tomorrow I'll give you the phone back."

6

Espinosa spent the day waiting for a phone call or some other contact with Celeste. He went out to have lunch by himself, settling on the Galeria Menescal. It took him longer than usual to eat his falafel sandwich and drink his soft drink. He decided to head back to work via the Avenida Copacabana, which at that hour was full of people. That would make it easier for Celeste to approach him if she had a mind to try. She didn't.

He thought it was unlikely that she'd call the station. He was surprised to pick up the phone and hear a feminine voice at the other end of the line.

"Officer?"

"Celeste?"

"Who's Celeste?"

"Who's this?"

"Serena."

"Serena! Sorry, I was thinking about . . ."

"Celeste. Men are always thinking about women, almost always some other woman."

"That's exactly what was happening, but it's not what you think."

"Of course not. But I'm not calling to talk about another woman. Do you want to meet me tonight, at six? I promise we won't be going to an AA meeting."

"Sure, but as I said yesterday, there's always the possibility that something might come up. How are you?"

"Fine. Nothing's going to come up. Take down this address."

When he'd written it down, she said:

"It's also in Leme. You won't have any trouble finding the building."

Moments after Serena's call, Welber showed up in Espinosa's office. He looked like he'd just woken up. Espinosa led him over to the window, gave him the phone he'd dropped the night before, and the two spoke with their faces turned toward the loud corner of Barata Ribeiro.

"Tell me something, Welber. The woman you saw in the car last night—you said yourself it might have been a man dressed as a woman."

"True, but only as a possibility. I didn't think it was a man. Are you thinking about the murderer?"

"I am."

"It wasn't him."

"Why are you so sure?"

"Because it was such an amateur way to follow someone."

"Maybe that's what he wanted you to think."

"Sir, over the last few days you've only been watched by three people: the woman you met yesterday, the woman I saw in the car, and me. If anybody else was around, it was a specialist, a master of the trade."

"Maybe our man, besides being a master killer, has other skills as well. But what's important now is that Celeste is hiding. She must be terrified and is trying to get in touch. Maybe she'd seen you somewhere else some other time. No need to keep watch for the next couple of days. Let's give her a chance to get closer."

"That is, if what's keeping her away is the fact that she saw me, which I doubt. You're the boss, but I don't want you to be exposed."

"I'm not the one the murderer wants. He wants Celeste, and the only reason he'd be interested in me is if she comes looking for me. If she gets in touch, I'll call you and we'll come up with a plan to protect her."

It was ten to six when Espinosa left the station with a note in his pocket. On it was the address Serena had given him. The cab driver didn't mind the short trip, which Espinosa saw as a promising sign for the evening. When the taxi stopped at the address he'd given the driver, they were in front of Serena's building. Espinosa took out the paper and checked again. It wasn't the same building. It was an even number; her building's address was odd. He looked at the building across the street. That was the one. He looked back at his note. It was the same floor as Serena's own.

He gave the number to the doorman, who simply pointed to the elevator. He got off at the floor indicated and found the apartment. There was no need to ring the bell; the door was ajar. Serena was standing in the middle of the room in a simple dress. Espinosa felt genuinely befuddled. He was charmed by Serena's beauty but didn't understand what she was doing in the apartment, looking for all the world like she owned the place. She greeted him with a soft kiss on the lips, just as she had left him the night before, and took him to the window, where he could see a bit of the sea and the day's last rays of sun over the islands on the horizon. Directly in front of them was Serena's apartment.

"Isn't it incredible?" she said. "Now the roles have been reversed."

"What do you mean? What is all this? What are you doing in this apartment?"

"So many questions! Nothing's happening . . . except that we're alone here."

"What do you mean by all this?"

"Maybe I should ask you the same question."

The answer disconcerted Espinosa momentarily. Of course he had something in mind, or else he wouldn't have left work to meet a married woman at a place other than her home. Of course he had something in mind. Besides, she was beautiful and incredibly provocative in that dress, the straps of which barely seemed to hold it up. It was more than obvious what he'd had in mind.

Before he could think of something to say, Serena put her arms around his neck and said, "Relax, we're not in an AA meeting. It's just us here. I know it might look weird to you, but I'll explain everything. Let's have a seat."

"Whose apartment is this?"

"First let me tell you what I have to drink. Coffee, soft

drinks, tea, and water. I'm sorry, but in the home of an alcoholic you don't get real drinks."

"Thanks, I'm fine, for now. I'm trying to figure out what's going on here. Whose apartment is this?"

"I don't know who the owner is, but I rented it for a month."

"You rented it? But don't you live across the street?"

"That's exactly why I rented it. Now the roles are reversed."

"What do you mean by that?"

"I mean that from here I can see what's going on in my apartment across the street."

Espinosa got up, and Serena followed.

"Serena, please, make yourself clear."

"I'll explain. I said I saw what happened in this apartment. I saw the two fighting. I saw her throw her purse out the window. I saw the woman fall and hit the sidewalk. I saw someone take away the purse. That window there. He doesn't know how much I saw, but he must assume it was a lot. And: he must think I saw him throw her out of the window and that I could identify him. And if that's what he's thinking, he'll try to kill me. He knows where I live. Except that when he comes for me, I'll be here, looking at him."

"And you think a professional killer who in the last month has killed three policemen and three women is going to sit playing cat and mouse with you, running back and forth across the street?"

"If there's no other way . . ."

"But there is another way. All he has to do is cross the street and kill you."

"Not if you're there."

"What do you mean?"

"We can come up with a way to communicate quickly so I can warn you if he shows up. I won't be waiting for him to cross the street, and if he does I'm not going to sit here waiting for him to throw me out the window."

"Serena, he's not an amateur. He's a cold-blooded killer."

Espinosa looked at Serena, standing in front of him, without taking his eyes off her cleavage or her legs, and tried to think rationally about what she'd said.

"Your eyes are telling me something," she said.

"What?"

"They're asking a question."

"What question?"

"They're asking what would happen if I slipped out of my dress."

"And what would happen?"

Serena removed the two shoulder straps and let the dress slide to the floor. She was stark naked.

7

When he got back to his apartment at eleven that night, the answering machine registered three calls, but there were no messages. While he was in the shower, he listened for the phone, but it didn't ring.

The next day at the station, at close to ten in the morning, he called Welber and invited him for coffee around the corner. But before they'd even made it down the stairs they doubled back to his office.

"This is ridiculous. We don't need to go around the corner, we can talk right here."

"Either way, Chief. I've already gotten used to our coworkers and their nasty looks. What happened?"

"Do you think Artur is trustworthy?"

"I think so. What do you want from him?"

"I want you two to be on duty this weekend."

Espinosa told the story of Serena, omitting certain intimate details and emphasizing her decision to set herself up as bait for the killer.

"Which means that as of today we have two women as probable future victims," Espinosa concluded.

"How is she going to attract him?"

"She doesn't have to do anything. She thinks the murderer saw her when he threw the woman out of the window."

"And did he?"

"She didn't see him push her, but she saw the two fighting before the woman threw her purse out and then fell. She thinks he'll try to silence her."

"Why hasn't he tried already?"

"Because he's been too busy trying to find Celeste."

"Sir, do you think someone who's killed six people is worried about being identified by a witness who was in another building, across the street, fifty feet away, at night?"

"Maybe. Cop killers have a tough time of it. He might be wanting to protect himself. So much that he still hasn't let himself be seen."

"And what do you want us two to do?"

"I want you both to have cell phones on you at all times, for our use only. I need to be able to reach you night and day, and I need you to be able to get to where I need you to go immediately. I can get the phones for you today."

"Artur and I both have cars."

"Great. I'll give you a gas allowance. One of the women lives in Leme. Her name is Serena. She's married to a big shot in the federal government, and her temporary address is the apartment the woman was thrown out of, on the tenth floor. The other is Celeste, who has disappeared. Tell Artur and nobody else."

"Why is the address of the woman married to the government big shot the same as the murdered woman's?"

"Long story. Her real address is in the building across the street. I just gave you the temporary one."

"Another question, sir. Is she the same one who was at the AA meeting?"

"She is."

"You told me to tell Artur. Do you mean everything?"

"Some of it you can keep under your hat."

He spent the time remaining before lunch getting his hands on a couple of phones for Welber and Artur. Right before he left, he got the call he had been expecting for days.

"Espinosa? It's Celeste. How about lunch at the Arabic place?"

"Great idea."

"In ten minutes, is that all right?"

"Perfect."

He put on his coat and left without speaking to anyone. He took the Rua Barata Ribeiro, the shortest way to the Galeria Menescal. Celeste wasn't at the restaurant but at a store at the corner of the gallery. As soon as he walked by, she grabbed his arm, and they jumped into the nearest taxi. The same tactic he'd used the first time. After confirming that they weren't being followed, Espinosa suggested a restaurant downtown that was pleasant enough and had a side entrance as well as a principal one. Celeste had cut her hair short and dyed it blond. She was wearing small, round sunglasses and one of the dresses Irene had given her.

"Sorry about disappearing like that."

"What happened?"

"People started asking questions at the hotel."

"Who? Asking what?"

"Must have been the cops. Asking if there were any women there alone. Luckily the manager interpreted it a different way and said that the hotel didn't accept unaccompanied women."

"Where did you go?"

"To another hotel."

"What are you going to do?"

"Same as I've done until now. Until I can carry out my plan."

"What plan?"

"I've already done the first part. Now I have to do the second. But before I explain, I have to ask if you're going to get my lunch. I haven't eaten very well lately."

"Sorry. Of course."

Espinosa got the waiter's attention. Only then did he look around at the restaurant and the other guests. It was a quiet place with wood-paneled walls, small beveled-glass windows, and pleasant lighting, frequented by lawyers and executives from foreign corporations. At this hour there were few people. Espinosa asked for the menu and they ordered—or, rather, they accepted the waiter's suggestions. While waiting for their food, Celeste described her plan for escaping her death sentence.

"I think you've already found out that Nestor, Ramos, and Silveira were involved in funneling bribes to policemen. Over the last few years, I'd accompanied Nestor to the meetings he held to distribute the money. They were almost always in his apartment in Copacabana. Since I was always there, I figured out who got what and how much. It wasn't the same amount for everyone. The chiefs got most of it and the lower-ranking officers less. Even so, everyone doubled or tripled their salaries that way. In the last few days, when I've been hiding, I had time to write it all down, with the names of all the beneficiaries. The list includes precinct chiefs and prison guards and even a few politicians. I wrote down names, amounts, dates, places, and means of delivery—even, in a few cases, the things they bought with the money. I made five copies of the dossier and deposited them in a bank, together with an authorization to deliver them to the five people whose names are on the envelopes. After that, I found a lawyer and had him draw up an agreement to deliver them to the addressees in case I should be attacked, die suspiciously, or disappear. The five are all people I know, and they all have access to the media. You are one of them. Your role is to let policemen know that these lists exist."

"Very clever . . . and dangerous."

"What's the danger?"

"It's like telling every station in town that you've got a load of dynamite that could blow up the building, and that five people—six, including you—have the key to detonate it. It's not a potential threat, it's a real one."

"So?"

"So they're not going to sit back and pray for you not to change your mind. What if you decide to stir things up a little by distributing the envelopes anyway?"

"What do you think they can do? There's no alternative."

The waiter arrived with their food. Espinosa found it hard to eat after that conversation, but he was gratified to see Celeste throw herself at the clay pot holding the seafood paella.

After lunch, they discussed other possible reactions to the news. Espinosa still thought it was risky, though he acknowledged that he couldn't come up with anything better.

"Think about it, Espinosa. It's either that or having to change my name, my city, my face, and disappear from the face of the earth. What difference would it make then if I was physically dead?"

"You already deposited the envelopes in the bank?"

"I did."

"So you're not asking for my opinion. The decision's already been made."

"It has. It was my choice."

"You know I'm going to try to get the list."

"I can imagine. That's why I didn't tell you the name of the bank it's kept in. I also don't think you're going to be able to get a court order to investigate bank by bank, branch by branch. There's thousands of them."

"I wasn't thinking of getting a court order. I was thinking of getting it from you."

"Espinosa, that list is my salvation."

"In any case, I'm going to try. While the news gets around, where are you going to be?"

"I'm not going to stay in one place for more than two

days. The hard part is that the options for my budget in the Zona Sul are running out. I don't want to go to areas I'm not familiar with; that would make me even more nervous."

Celeste had eaten enough for both of them. He gazed admiringly at the woman in front of him, who, persecuted by the police force itself, had managed, all on her own, to come up with a strategy to neutralize even her fiercest pursuers.

"You needed that, after all those days in hiding."

"I think it's going to work."

"I was referring to the paella."

"Ah! And it was delicious!"

"So now we can think about dessert."

"Ice cream! I'd love some mango ice cream."

With her new look, Celeste stood out from the other diners. The restaurant had filled up since they'd come in. She was not entirely relaxed, but she had let down her guard enough to be able to enjoy the pleasant ambience as well as the food. As she shared her bowl of ice cream with Espinosa, she entertained him with anecdotes about her quick moves over the last few days.

"What are you going to do until the news gets around?"

"Stay hidden for another week, here in Rio. Then I'm thinking about spending some time elsewhere, maybe a smaller city where things are more affordable. I've scraped together every cent I could. It'll be enough for a month or two, depending on where I end up. Then I'll think about what to do next. First I want to see the effect of the news."

"While you're doing that, try not to go out unnecessarily."

Celeste stretched her arms across the table and took Espinosa's hand.

"You've been really great to me. How are you going to break the news?"

"I'm going to say that I got a call from a lawyer telling me about the dossier in the bank."

"Perfect."

8

After putting Celeste in a cab, Espinosa called the group to arrange a meeting that afternoon. At three, Ramiro, Welber, and Artur sat in a semicircle around the chief's desk.

"There's no need to look out for Celeste anymore," Espinosa began.

"Was she . . ." Welber swallowed the rest of the question.

"No, she wasn't killed. I had lunch with her, and I can guarantee that she's alive."

"Did they get the man?"

"No. But I think he'll have to give up. Which doesn't mean we're going to give up trying to get him."

Espinosa filled them in on his meeting with Celeste and her plan to get the murderer off her back. He added that he'd gotten a call from the lawyer confirming the existence of the envelopes and the fact that his name was among the recipients.

"Nobody, not even the lawyer, has access to the list, unless Celeste dies or is attacked. According to what she told me, the list is perfectly complete. She didn't give me any names."

"Why didn't the people who died do the same?"

"Maybe they didn't understand why the murders were happening, or they didn't have time to come up with an effective defense. Don't forget that almost every cop equates defense with firepower. Celeste decided to use her head."

"If it works, we'll have an even smaller chance of getting the killer," Ramiro said.

"But that's not the idea," Espinosa answered. "The possibility that Celeste might be out of danger doesn't mean that we're going to let up on trying to get the guy who killed three cops and three women right beneath our noses. He'll probably leave town, realizing that he might himself be killed, to prevent him from snitching—even though I don't think the people who ordered the killing have had direct contact with him. In any case, he'll be out of circulation."

Espinosa kept the meeting going for another few minutes, reinforcing in his colleagues' minds how crucial the dossier was to Celeste's hopes of survival. It was three-forty when the meeting ended. He was sure that by the end of the afternoon everyone in his station would have heard about the dossier. By the end of the weekend, every policeman in Rio would know.

9

Serena was lying on the couch in her temporary apartment, thinking about the evening before with Espinosa, there, in that same room, in the fading light. Better and worse than she'd imagined: he was in better shape than she'd thought, but he wasn't one for romance. He was a man of action. His problem wasn't incurable; he was just a little out of touch with what women want. Nothing she couldn't handle.

The meeting with Espinosa brought back memories of the days when she'd sung in bars and clubs. A policeman and a nightclub singer could fit into the same photo album, but it would be hard to sneak them into the Rodes family album, along with pictures of their son graduating from Harvard. Luckily, the officer clearly hadn't interpreted the rendezvous as the beginning of a romance. She wanted an adventure. She didn't want romance. She could always have that with her husband, since romance was always pretend anyway.

Every minute or so she got up and looked out the window. It wasn't just the window across the way that attracted her attention; she was also interested in the street and the people on the sidewalks. She was sure she could identify the murderer if she saw him, even though she'd only glimpsed him from a distance on the night of the crime. It wasn't his appearance she expected to recognize. It was more a feeling that had passed between them. He probably hadn't seen her very clearly. The light was behind her, and he couldn't have focused on her face for more than a second. But he had the advantage of knowing where she lived. Which was why she was waiting.

PART 4

1

The airplane landed at Santos Dumont just after seven. Irene called Espinosa from the arrivals area, trying him first at the station and then at his apartment. He'd already left the one and still hadn't made it to the other. She got in a taxi and decided not to try him again until she got home.

Not much had happened over the last two days, nothing that required his direct involvement. Sometimes on Friday, the tide turned: not much action during the day, but then the flow of incidents increased at night, reaching a climax in the early-morning hours. It was usually street kids robbing tourists, prostitutes, and transvestites, or drunken brawls in bars and nightclubs. They could fill him in on all of it later. He left the station at six.

He hadn't seen Irene in almost a week. The time had been filled by Celeste and Serena, Serena occupying most of it. She wasn't a substitute for Irene, and he didn't mean her to be, either.

While he was walking down the busy sidewalk—he'd chosen the new route, past the bookstore—he thought about how hard it was to adhere to a consistent sexual morality. What were you supposed to do when you were alone with a beautiful woman who stripped and stared at you like an ice-cream cone staring at a kid on a hot summer day?

Naturally, he was looking for a justification. He wasn't a kid, and Serena wasn't an ice-cream cone. And it wasn't a matter of making an ethical decision. What was done was done; he'd fallen into a sexual trap and there was no way he could have escaped. He didn't feel guilty about Irene: they had never agreed not to see other people. She'd never asked if he'd been with other women, and he'd never asked what she did on her free evenings in São Paulo (or even in Rio). Whatever they did on their own had no bearing on the enormous pleasure they shared when they were together.

There was nothing novel in that reflection. He wasn't weighing the pros and cons. The truth was, the situation suited both of them perfectly. He already knew that. So why was he thinking about it? If he missed Irene, all he had to do was call her. Why keep drooping along like that, hands in his pockets, eyes gazing off into the distance, with an entirely unjustified feeling of emptiness?

It was in that state that he arrived at the bookstore. For the first time, he was interested not in the books but in the store itself. He studied the window and the sale table outside, wondering if that's how he would have arranged them or if he'd have tried to think of something else. Both items—the window and the sale table—were essential to attracting customers. As for the interior, he would definitely have tried to make it more attractive, more charming. Mentally, he moved things around and conjured more inviting shelving.

"May I help you, sir?"

"Thanks, I'm just having a look."

"I'm here if you need anything."

Espinosa examined a few shelves and looked at their foreign literature section, pausing in front of an old Jules Verne collection, the same one he'd had since his teens. Published in Portugal by the Livraria Bertrand, they were wine-colored hardbacks with black-and-white illustrations. He tried to remember where they were in his living room. The feeling of the binding and the paper brought back memories of adventures on the Mysterious Island and the sensation of being trapped on the *Nautilus*. He left the store, walked another block, and, before heading home, strolled through the Galeria Menescal.

So that was it: his life was becoming monotonous, repetitive, and the visit to the bookstore only made him feel it more keenly. He was walking away from the Arabic restaurant with his take-out meatballs; even they expressed the dullness of his life. He thought about getting something else, but then decided against it. Spaghetti and meatballs: that was his dinner. That was what his life had become. He didn't need to change too radically—he could still enjoy used books and Middle Eastern cuisine—but he did need to break the tedium of his days. It wasn't just a matter of taking a different route to work; he needed to find a different route through life.

Back at home, he checked the answering machine, transferred the frozen spaghetti from the package to a plate, left the meatballs wrapped up so they wouldn't get cold, and got in the shower. When the phone rang, a little after seven, he was lathering up his hair.

2

Serena was waiting for her husband, not realizing that he'd arrived that morning and headed straight to Brasília. A meeting with the minister to update him on the meetings in Washington, he now called to say. He'd be back the next day. Serena turned on the light in her dressing room, went downstairs, crossed the street, and entered the other building. She didn't turn on any lights. She simply walked up to the windowsill in order to spy on her own illuminated room. She didn't look at the street; she imagined the murderer leaning against a lamppost, pretending to read a newspaper, as in an old detective movie. But this wasn't a movie. That a woman had been thrown out of the window, only a couple of weeks earlier, from the same window where she now stood was tragically real. She should have brought her binoculars so she could see his face in detail. She imagined his surprise when, looking up at the window from which he'd thrown the woman, he'd catch a glimpse of a face staring at him. Maybe he'd just notice the glint off the binoculars. She didn't have a watch, but the TVs in the other apartments announced the beginning and the end of an evening soap opera, between eight and nine. The same time that the woman had been killed. Her maid would be off duty, having gone down to the Avenida Atlântica to flirt. Her apartment was entirely available to the killer.

From her vantage point—seated in a chair, not too close to the window, with all the lights off—she could study her own apartment without being seen by anybody else. She shifted her gaze to the sea, the street, the entrance to her building, repeating the sequence innumerable times before noticing that the light she had left on in her dressing room had been turned off. She felt slightly giddy. Maybe Zuleide had checked the lights before leaving. She slowly calmed herself down, though she was still out of breath. She looked back at her apartment. It was completely dark. She sheltered her eyes from the lights coming from the street and the other buildings, trying to make out something in the darkness of her dressing room. She lost track of time: one minute, ten minutes . . . she couldn't say. Suddenly, she had the clear impression of a little point of red light—like someone removing a cigarette from their mouth after taking a drag. She couldn't see anything else in her dressing room, but she was absolutely certain that a man was peering at her from the darkness. She felt dizzy again, this time more so, as if on the verge of fainting. She gripped the sides of the chair, thinking that she had to do something before she passed out. She found the card next to the phone, went into the bathroom, and turned on the light to read the number. She went back into the living room and called Espinosa.

Italian spaghetti, Arabic meatballs: it wasn't exactly haute cuisine. It occurred to Espinosa that he should have

gotten something German to round out the culinary fu-
sion. He was removing the spaghetti from the microwave
when the phone rang. He quickly answered, imagining
that it was Irene suggesting a real dinner.

It was a woman's voice, but not Irene's. It took him a
minute to recognize it.

"Espinosa?"

"Speaking."

"I need you to come immediately!"

"Who—"

"It's Serena, I can see the murderer—he's in the apartment—"

"Where are you?"

"In the apartment. He's there, I'm sure of it."

"You're in your apartment?"

"No, I'm in the one I rented. He got there . . . turned out
the light I'd left on. I kept looking, he was smoking . . ."

"Your husband—"

"My husband's in Brasília. He doesn't smoke."

"Nobody else is in your apartment?"

"The maid. . . . She left. . . . She doesn't smoke either."

"You're sure someone's there?"

"Fuck yes, someone's there!"

"I'm on my way. Stay where you are and don't do anything."

He looked at the dinner on the table, picked up a meat-
ball, and left. He didn't think it was worth mobilizing Welber and Artur.

On the first try, the car's motor groaned. He tried a second time; it barely muttered. The third time it didn't even speak. He locked the car and got in a cab.

As soon as Irene got home, she listened to the week's messages. There weren't many; one of them was from Espinosa asking if she'd gotten back. Then she skimmed the mail: a few bills, two letters. She emptied her suitcase and took a slow, relaxing shower. Still wrapped in her towel, she called Espinosa. The same laconic answering-machine message greeted her. She ordered Japanese, turned on the TV, and began to think she might as well have stayed in São Paulo.

3

The taxi arrived at its destination ten minutes after the phone call. Espinosa looked up at the buildings, one across from the other, and saw that both of Serena's apartments were dark.

He walked past the doorman, who greeted him, certainly recognizing him from two days earlier, and headed toward the elevator. He gathered from the doorman's unperturbed manner that nothing out of the ordinary had transpired on the tenth floor, at least nothing like what had happened a couple of weeks ago. As soon as she heard the ring of the doorbell, followed by Espinosa's voice, Serena opened the door.

She looked genuinely terrified. She took the policeman's arm and led him to the middle of the room, at a prudent distance from the window.

"That one's my dressing room," she said, pointing at the building across the way. "There was someone there. I saw."

"There was nobody home when you left?"

"Zuleide, the maid, but she left right after me."

"Your husband might have come back from Brasília early."

"I called the doorman. He's not back."

"What did you see?"

"A man taking a cigarette out of his mouth."

"You saw that?"

"I saw the end of the cigarette and then saw him take it out of his mouth."

"And you saw that it was a man?"

"Who is going to go into my apartment at night and smoke a cigarette?"

"That's what I was going to ask."

"The only people with keys are Guilherme and Zuleide. Besides me, of course."

"You don't think it's a little odd that someone would break into your apartment at night to smoke?"

"I think it was on purpose . . . for me to see. . . . He knew I was here."

"That doesn't make sense. If he knew you were here, why didn't he come over here to get you?"

"What the fuck! Are you interrogating me? Who knows why he didn't come here! I almost think you would have liked it better that way."

"I'm trying to find out if you really saw him or if you just think you saw him."

"Of course I saw him!"

"You saw something that looked like the lit end of a cigarette. It could have been a reflection."

"The window is open; there was nowhere for it to reflect. Besides, I didn't just see the lit end, I also saw it move."

"So let's go check it out."

"Go there?"

"Isn't that what you wanted? Isn't that why you rented this place? Isn't that why you called me?"

"Fine. Let's go."

The elevator was still on their floor. They went down, crossed the street, and entered her building.

"Good evening, Dona Serena."

"Good evening, Raimundo. Did anyone ask for me?"

"I just got here. But no one's come by, ma'am."

"Has Dr. Guilherme gotten back?"

"No, ma'am."

"And Zuleide?"

"She already left."

Before going up, Espinosa asked Serena to describe the apartment: the layout of the rooms, the location of the service entrance, rooms that she kept locked. He wanted to go in without turning on the lights.

"If you enter in the dark, I should go with you to show you around."

"Wait for me down here."

"But I want to go with you."

"Negative. Stay here with the doorman."

"Why can't I go up?"

"You'd be in the way."

"And what if he leaves and finds me here?"

"He won't. I'll buzz down when you can come up."

He took her key and went up. He didn't believe anyone was in the apartment, which is why he hadn't called Welber and Artur. Nobody broke into an apartment at night and smoked. If the intruder wanted to be seen, he could have turned on the lights. Just in case, he opened the door soundlessly. He didn't need to adjust to the dark; the wide living room boasted twenty feet of windows that reflected the streetlights from the Avenida Atlântica. Espinosa stood for a minute looking around and listening carefully. He was impressed by how many noises there could be in an empty apartment, and how many little green and red lights there were blinking on different electronic apparatuses.

The room was too bright for anyone to hide there. He could make out the beginning of the hallway leading to the other rooms of the apartment. The darkness blurred the distances. He didn't know whether the hall was long or short, and he couldn't tell where the doors were. From Serena's description, he knew that the first door on the right was the bathroom. He confirmed this, then calculated the distance to the other rooms and began to check these out one by one. He paid special attention not only to what he could see and hear but also to what he could smell. After examining the service area, he proceeded through the bedrooms and bathrooms, until he reached the dressing room. Only then did he turn on the lights and walk back through the apartment. Nobody. He called Serena on the intercom.

"He ran off?" Serena asked as soon as Espinosa opened the door for her.

"Nobody was there. The apartment was empty and in perfect order."

"I want to go to the dressing room."

"Sure. Let's go."

They stood in the middle of the room, Serena gripping Espinosa's arm tightly.

"There's one more thing," he said. "I didn't smell smoke, and there aren't any ashes anywhere."

Serena exhaled, relieved, and loosened her grip on the policeman's arm. When she looked across the street, however, she cried out.

"It was off!"

"What was off?"

"The light in the living room! It was off when we were there, and we left it off! Now it's on! He saw us leave and went over there."

"What are you saying?"

"I'm saying that he saw I wasn't alone and decided not to attack me."

"Maybe."

"That's it?"

"Or maybe you were just under the impression that you saw him in the first place."

"And the woman thrown out of the window, that was just an impression? Maybe you standing here—just an impression!"

"What I'm saying is that all this is only based on the fact that you think you saw a lit cigarette fifty or sixty feet away. You could have perfectly well been mistaken."

"True. And I could have perfectly well been mistaken about you. . . . I'm nervous. Let's have a seat in the living room. Do you want a drink?"

"Thanks, I still haven't had dinner . . . and I don't re-member having lunch either."

"Will you walk me to the other apartment? That light is scaring me."

"Sure."

For the second time that night, they crossed the street toward the other apartment. The door was locked, the light was still on, and there was no sign of anybody's having been there.

"Before you closed the door, you might have hit the light switch. People do it automatically. You were scared . . ."

"Maybe. Sorry. I was rude to you. Do you want to stay here? We could order some food."

"I have to go home."

Serena turned off the light. They went out, then crossed the street together for the third time.

It was ten-thirty when Espinosa got home and saw the spaghetti and meatballs on the table. He put the whole thing in the microwave. His appetite was only heightened by the dinner. At least there was still an old beer in the fridge.

4

He devoted Saturday morning to checking on his car's battery. He'd try to recharge it; there was no reason to buy a new one and ruin that one as well. It wouldn't take long; he'd still have time to finish reading the papers. The most difficult part was finding someone to help him jump-start the car. Once that was done, the rest was easy. He didn't even lose an hour. He did lose some money: the battery couldn't be salvaged. Back home, with the car and its new battery parked in its usual place, he picked up the papers and drank his coffee, allowing himself an extra cup and two pieces of toast. On the answering machine, there was a silent message. He thought about Celeste. Irene would have left a message or hung up before the beep. Serena . . . the night before had ended on such a melancholy note.

Still those three: Celeste, Irene, Serena. And on this Saturday morning he thought he'd performed heroically by taking care of the car first thing. He was past forty, an age when emotions become less pronounced, but he was still far from sixty. Being satisfied with toast and sugar-free jam on a beautiful Saturday morning in the middle of summer in Rio de Janeiro: was that how it was supposed to be? He had nothing against toast and jam. It just seemed odd that that was all the company he had this morning. That and the papers. He'd already taken the car for a walk.

He didn't finish the papers. He put on shorts, a T-shirt, tennis shoes, and a cotton hat he'd had for several decades, and took a walk down the Avenida Atlântica. He didn't want to walk in the sand. On the weekends it was impossible to take three steps on the beach without bumping into half a dozen people. The sidewalk wasn't exactly deserted, but at least he could move. He walked the five blocks that separated the Peixoto District from the beach, arriving almost exactly halfway down the Avenida Atlântica. He crossed the road and found the sidewalk, veering left, toward the Rock of Leme. If he had been in good shape he would have covered the entire length of the beach; instead he did half of it and went home. At eleven on a midsummer morning, he could take being outside only if he were right next to the water, so he could jump in every once in a while. When he got home, there were two messages: the first, from Irene, reported that she was back in Rio. The second was silent. He called Irene. She'd gone out.

He had lunch at the Italian place, his usual Saturday hangout. To make up for the disappointing meal the night before, he had a risotto with red wine. When he left the restaurant, the afternoon was halfway over and people were leaving the beach, tugging their children and all their beach paraphernalia after them. The walk to the Peixoto District was leisurely, giving him time to burn off the wine and digest the risotto. The bookstore was right on the way to his house, but he decided to take a slight detour to avoid it. At the end of the afternoon he picked up *Phan-*

tom Lady again—he still wasn't even to the hundred and fourth day before the execution.

None of the three women called. Not until the next day, in the evening, the weekend almost over, did he manage to speak to Irene.

"Maybe we could meet up in São Paulo?" she said. "I have to go back tomorrow."

"If we must . . ."

"We don't *must*, dear, but it might actually be interesting. It's not the most romantic city in the world, but it's hundreds of miles from the Twelfth Precinct."

On Monday morning, Espinosa was thinking about Celeste's gambit. He wondered how long it would protect her. He knew that by now everyone involved would have heard about the dossiers and called off their hired guns. When he got to the station, there was a message from her suggesting lunch at A Polaca, not fifty feet from the station and often full of cops.

Fifteen minutes before the arranged time, Espinosa went to the restaurant to wait for her.

"You couldn't have picked a more exposed place," he said when she arrived.

"You know how in poker you can show all your cards but one? That's what I'm doing. I'm not going to spend the rest of my days with my tail between my legs."

"It's risky."

"Dating a policeman is risky too. I learned that a long time ago."

"Having lunch with a policeman is also risky."

"Not when the policeman's honest. And everyone knows who is and who isn't. Without officers like you, the police department couldn't justify its existence and would drop dead. They need you a lot more than you know."

"So you think I'm a good card in your hand?"

"Espinosa, I'm not playing with you."

The decision to come out of hiding had done wonders for Celeste. She was well-groomed, nicely dressed, and, considering the circumstances, as calm as possible.

"Why are you looking at me like that?"

"Because you're so pretty."

"Thanks. Over these last few days I've had plenty of time to take care of myself. This morning I went to my apartment. I could put on my own clothes and be in my own home, even if only for a short time. If you can't do that, it's not worth living. I sent your friend's clothes to the cleaners. If you give me her address, I'd like to send her a thank-you note."

"Do you feel safe at home?"

"Not yet, but I can't keep living in cheap hotels, exposed to all kinds of dangers, without my own clothes and my own things, without a little comfort. . . . You can do it for a couple of weeks, but then it becomes a prison. I don't know if I'm safer at home or in a hotel. If they decide to kill me, they'll find a way sooner or later. But I don't think they'll do it. The fact is, I don't feel safe enough yet to move back home. I'm going to give it some time. A month or two, like I said. With the money I have left, I can take a break for a few weeks, somewhere a little more remote."

During the meal a lot of eyes were on them. If someone still didn't know about the dossiers, they would after that lunch. The cards were on the table. Everyone knew that Celeste had come out of hiding and that a nonaggression pact had been signed. As long as it was respected, the list wouldn't be made public. Espinosa put Celeste in a cab after she promised to stay in touch.

"Send me a postcard," he joked. "When you get back, we'll have lunch again."

Celeste gave Espinosa a warm kiss, and the taxi took off.

By the Avenida Atlântica on Tuesday morning, the high waves had swallowed half the sand on the beach. The waves were frightening even from a safe distance, and nobody was sitting on the little strip of surviving sand. Tourists hated days like that, but not Espinosa. He walked down the sidewalk admiring the same sea where, thirty years before, his father had taught him to swim. Neither the violence of the waves nor the wind that whipped up their foam bothered Espinosa; they were both old friends. Something else was bothering him.

Back at the station, the only event out of the ordinary was a call from Serena, apologizing for Friday night.

"It might have been my imagination," she said.

"I hope so. What about the light in the other apartment?"

"Maybe you're right, maybe I did hit the switch on the way out. It's an old habit, even though I thought I'd notice if the light went on. But nothing else happened, and that's what's important."

"Is your husband back?"

"He is. He didn't like that I'd rented the apartment; he didn't understand why."

"To be honest, I don't either."

"Maybe I'm not sure myself . . . but it doesn't matter. I can leave the apartment locked up until the end of the month, when the lease runs out, or I can just hand it back over. Thanks for your help."

She hung up without another word.

The group's next meeting, scheduled for noon, was held in the chief's office. No special security measures were taken. The three detectives sat in the three available chairs; two others were loaded down with paperwork and files.

"And?" Espinosa asked Ramiro.

The inspector spoke in his capacity as chief of the detectives.

"We don't see any reason to hold the meetings anywhere else. Certain things don't need to be dealt with as carefully anymore."

"Such as?"

"Celeste. She's no longer hiding, and everyone knows what she did. We don't need to go somewhere else to talk about her."

"Which doesn't necessarily mean that she's thrown off the murderer."

"We don't think he'll try anything else." Ramiro paused. "But there's something else, sir. Our investigation no longer makes sense. Our colleagues are saying that if she really has this dossier, it's because she knows who was getting money but isn't going to say. They say the secret's safe as long as she's alive. And that she's your friend, since she had lunch with you yesterday—they also say you had lunch with her last week—which means that you agree with what she's doing."

"And?"

"And so what are we investigating?"

"You're investigating six murders: three of our colleagues and three people associated with them, deaths that you yourself have linked to the underground lottery."

"That was before Celeste did what she did, sir."

"No. Absolutely not. Celeste did something to save her own life. She was the next victim of the murderer. The only reason she wasn't killed already is that he got the two women mixed up. The pact between her and the murderer has nothing to do with anyone but her. They could tell the murderer to finish her off today, and we have to protect her. Let's make a couple of things clear: first, Celeste is the victim. If she did what she did, it's only because we couldn't guarantee her safety by getting the killer. Second, I don't have any dossier or any list. Third, I didn't agree to do anything with anyone. Finally, I didn't tell you to call off the investigation. Am I making myself clear?"

"Yes, sir," Ramiro answered.

"Anything else?"

"We learned something about the car ring."

"What?"

"I thought it was a red herring, but it wasn't. It looks like Nestor, Ramos, and Silveira really did have a car business, and it wasn't legit: they stole cars and defrauded insurers. Interestingly, the people who gave me this information were the same ones who wouldn't say a word about the lottery money."

"Which means that the information doesn't threaten them."

"We're trying to learn more."

"Then get back to work."

Espinosa's evening walk home was plagued with doubts about the police force. Why work for an institution whose members viewed honesty as a manufacturing defect similar to those that plagued automobiles? He imagined a department whose duty was to purge the force of those members whose ethics were out of sync with the rest of the company.

As he walked into his apartment the phone began to ring.

"I thought you'd be getting in about now." It was Serena.

"You were as precise as a Swiss watch."

"How terrible!"

"How are you?"

"Fine, but yesterday when we spoke I wasn't feeling well."

"What was the matter?"

"Insecurity. I was insecure about you, so I made that nice polite call to show you that I accepted that I might have made a mistake, that I might be a little flaky . . . that sort of thing."

"And now?"

"Now I'd like you to forget everything I said yesterday. I might have been wrong about seeing someone smoking in my apartment—I'll admit that the conditions weren't so favorable and I was really high-strung—but there was nothing like that on the night I saw the woman thrown out of the window. I was perfectly calm, and I saw the woman fighting with someone else. I agree that I couldn't see the other person so well, but he was there. And he saw me. He saw that I was watching. If the guy thinks I saw him throw the woman out of the window, he'll want to get rid of me. I didn't rent the apartment because I'm off my rocker, I rented it because I thought I was safer over there than in my own home. Especially when Guilherme's traveling. So I'm calling to say that I'm sticking to the story I told you when we first met."

"I never doubted that. I still think everything you said was very important."

"You're so sweet . . . and I miss you. Maybe we could have another meeting."

5

That night, he picked up his book again; he hadn't made it past the third chapter over the weekend. He wasn't sure he could focus on it. He was still thinking about Serena's phone call. Not just the last one either, but the disconnect between the last two, which so vividly illustrated the conflict between the two Serenas. He liked her, though he was a little put off by her impulsiveness. She seemed to deal with reality through fantasies. Serena wasn't a dreamer, and she didn't seem to believe in happiness; for her, the real danger wasn't so much unhappiness as boredom.

He went back over the events that had led him to Serena, searching for the improbable relation between the first call, when she wanted to discuss the dead woman, and the deaths under investigation. One coincidence bothered him more than anything else: Serena in the bar downtown and Serena calling to discuss the so-called suicide.

He didn't believe in coincidences like that, especially when it was a question of six murders. On the other hand, only an extremely paranoid mind could think that a random encounter in one of the busiest places in Rio could foreshadow six crimes. Even more improbable: five crimes and a suicide. He couldn't imagine what the connection between the two meetings could possibly be. Except for Celeste, the murderer's target. Serena had declared that the suicide was actually a murder; but only Celeste could tell them, as in fact she had, that the murderer had killed the wrong person. The logic of the crime made it easy, even imperative, to eliminate Celeste. Without her, the connection between the two series of murders disappeared, along with the last witness to the illicit activities of the three dead cops.

Sitting in his rocking chair, he looked out at the nearby hills. He saw the buildings across the square, and behind them São João Hill, where the lights ran all the way to the top of the Ladeira dos Tabajaras. It wasn't the most stunning view in the world, but during the day he enjoyed the sight of the green hills and the blue sky. Now, though, it was night. It was a little windy, but he didn't want to close the windows and he didn't feel like getting up. The next day was Wednesday, the maid's day. If the wind brought a few leaves inside, she would be able to sweep them up; she was very proud of her professional competence and felt useless when the house was overly clean.

He turned back to his book, but his concentration didn't last long. He couldn't put his finger on what was bothering him. It wasn't a thing, or a person, but a breakdown in logic. He sat in the rocking chair, with his open book resting on his lap, until he started to nod off. Then got up and went to bed. His eyes were tired, but it took him a long time to fall asleep.

Back at the station, things were still uneasy. Ever since the investigations had begun, the other cops had proven extremely defensive in their conversations with the task force. The three were ostracized not only in their own precinct but everywhere else as well. They received absolutely no help at all. There was some pro forma cooperation in each precinct, but the police force as a whole offered the same polite nonhelp. This second level included the chief of police, the secretary of security, and even the state governor. But what was happening in Espinosa's own precinct was up to him to fix. He called a general meeting of every policeman under his command, including those who weren't on duty that day, and ordered them to appear at five that afternoon.

At five on the dot, when the chief walked in the room, there were about thirty cops lounging around waiting for the meeting to begin. Only the couple of people working reception had been excused. As he walked to the front of the room, the chatting died down.

"This is not a general assembly," he began. "It's not a debate club. I called you here to say one thing. You all know that there is an investigation under way, conducted by Inspector Ramiro with the assistance of Detectives Welber and Artur. The goal of this investigation is to discover who murdered three of our colleagues and three of their friends. This investigation has already gone on for over a month, and if it was up to you people it'd go on for a year. The investigators have come across the same difficulty in other precincts. What matters to me, though, is what happens here. Obviously, the noncooperation they've faced is linked to facts the investigation has turned up about cor-

ruption in this station. I would like to make something perfectly clear. There is no such thing as a 'tip.' It is not an ad-
dition to your salary. Tips are corruption. And corruption,
besides being a legal problem, is also an ethical problem.
When it prevents us from discovering who killed your own
colleagues, the problem is extremely critical. I don't know
who among you is on the take, and I'm not going to turn
myself into an inquisitor. But I'm not going to let things
stay the way they are. As of today, even the tiniest sign that
you're on the take will unleash an immediate investigation, during which time you will lose your badge and the
right to bear arms until the conclusion of the investigation.
I won't hesitate to call in the attorney general's office, or to
send the cases up to the higher authorities. Whoever is up-
set by this decision has forty-eight hours to solicit a trans-
fer to another precinct. During this time all requests for
transfers will be processed and forwarded to the relevant
authorities. Get in touch with everyone who's not here and
tell them what I have said. That's it. Dismissed."

   In the first twenty-four hours, there was talk of getting
the whole precinct to ask for transfers, citing the chief's recent dictatorial behavior. At first the movement seemed to
have some momentum, but by the end of the second day
only half a dozen supporters remained. Once the grace pe-
riod was over, the few requests for transfers were immediately processed.
   Over those two days, Ramiro spoke to the widows once

again and heard references to certain garages where their husbands used to spend time. They didn't know the addresses. They knew only that the shops were in the sprawling, ramshackle Zona Oeste. With that information, Ramiro turned the screws on a couple of dealers in imported car parts and learned that the three cops had been supplying such parts for a long time. From people who dealt in shady cars in Rio and São Paulo, he learned that the cops weren't just weekend dealers: their business was international. The next week was entirely dedicated to discovering where their garages were located.

Espinosa thought that Celeste could help with this matter without breaking her code of silence, but Celeste had vanished. Welber and Artur's visits to her apartment in Botafogo met with the same response from the doormen: Dona Celeste had come back only once. She hadn't stayed more than half an hour and had left carrying a medium-sized leather bag.

"Was she alone?"

"She was."

"Did she seem nervous?"

"She seemed like she was in a hurry."

"Did you see if there was any car parked nearby, waiting for her?"

"No, sir. From here we can only see cars parked right in front of the buildings, and there's so much traffic around here that it'd be hard to say."

"What did she say when she left?"

"That she was going to be traveling for a few days."

"And how did she look?"

"Tough to say, sir, but not very comfortable."

"What do you mean?"

"She kept looking at the door."

The chief told the two young detectives to search for her in every one- and two-star hotel in the Zona Sul.

Espinosa suspected that the vague unpleasantness he'd been feeling all week had something to do with Serena. Right before the end of the day, he called her.

"Espinosa, darling, you guessed!"

"Guessed what?"

"That I wanted to talk to you. Well, I wanted to be with you. I mean, I also want to talk to you, but I want to do more than talk."

"And I want to talk to you," Espinosa answered.

"Did something else happen?"

"I hope not. Where do you want to talk?"

Serena said, "We could try the other apartment. I'm alone until Friday."

"I'll come by at six-thirty."

Daylight savings time had ended the day before. It was starting to get dark when Espinosa left the station and headed toward Leme. He had twenty minutes and decided to walk down the Avenida Copacabana. He liked walking with all the people going home from work.

He arrived five minutes early. He was welcomed with a long, tender hug and a more than tender kiss. He felt like a newlywed arriving after work to a greeting from his young spouse. He didn't like the idea, but he did like the feeling of Serena's body against his. She was wearing the same dress she'd had on last time, and Espinosa remembered the wonderful shamelessness with which she'd let it fall to the ground. Before that scene could be repeated, he walked her over to the window. They stood watching the sea as if waiting for a ship to come in. There weren't any ships; it was dark; and Espinosa wasn't the least bit interested in the view. He just wanted to take control of the situation.

"I wanted to talk a little about something you said last time."

"What do you want to know?"

"Are you sure you saw someone here besides Rosita?"

"Rosita?"

"The woman who lived here."

"Sure! I mean, I saw that someone was there, but I didn't see who it was; the lighting was bad. Even the woman, I wouldn't recognize her."

"Try to focus on the person who was with her. Close your eyes and describe the scene."

Serena sat down, closed her eyes, and waited silently. Then she began to speak.

"Two people talking in loud voices. No. Only one of them is talking. While they're talking, she's pacing across the room."

"You're sure she's talking?"

"I am. I could hear the voice. I just couldn't make out what she was saying."

"It couldn't have been the TV in someone's apartment? You said the first soap was on."

"Hmm . . . I don't think so. . . . She was moving her lips."

"You could see her lips moving?"

"I think so."

"And then?"

"Then I saw a purse fly out the window."

"If you couldn't see the people very well, why are you so sure it was a purse?"

"It wasn't a small purse, and I saw the strap perfectly in the light; I watched it fall to the ground. That's why I didn't see the murderer throwing the woman out. I was looking at the street, trying to see where the purse landed." Serena opened her eyes to look at Espinosa.

"That's fine. Close your eyes again. About this other person: what can you tell me about him?"

"The only thing I can say is that he was a little taller than the woman and was wearing a cap."

"You saw the cap?"

"I did. Against the light, the brim was easy to make out."

"What else?"

"I think he was wearing a jacket."

"Any other details?"

"After the woman fell, I looked up and thought he was looking at me. I looked down at the woman. When I looked back up, nobody was there. Why are you asking me all this again? To see if I'll contradict myself? You think I made it all up? You think the woman really killed herself? Is that it?"

"The more details you can give me, the stronger your story becomes."

"Fuck, Espinosa, it's not *my story!* I didn't make up something like that."

"All I have is your story. Nothing else."

"My big mistake was renting this apartment. Both you and my husband think it was crazy. You think I'm losing my mind when I say I saw the murderer again. The way you and Guilherme talk, you make me wonder what I really saw."

"Which is a good sign."

"I have no doubts about the basic story line."

"You do. You didn't see the man push Rosita out of the window, you aren't sure if they were talking or fighting, you don't know who threw out the purse, you don't know if the murderer really saw you. . . . The only thing you're sure about is that you saw the woman fall. And even there, you're not sure if she fell, if she jumped, or if she was pushed."

"Fell?"

"Why not? What if, during their discussion, one of them threw the purse at the other one, missed the target, and the purse fell out the window? Then Rosita ran to try to get it, slipped, and also fell out the window."

"You prick!"

"I'm not saying that's what happened, I'm just trying to show you that even though it may not be probable it's certainly *possible*."

"And they call me crazy."

"Sometimes reality can seem crazy."

"Fuck, Espinosa, you're not my shrink."

"Nor do I want to be."

6

It was already dark when Guilherme Rodes arrived home to find Serena in her dressing room, sitting in his swivel chair with the light out, staring at the building across the street. He'd thought it was just a passing phase, but it had become an obsession that occupied almost all of her time at home. He was no psychologist, but he knew that she was acting compulsively. He'd heard from the maid that Serena spent her afternoons in the other apartment, watching her own dressing room with binoculars. When she wasn't in one of the two apartments, she was at an AA meeting; she had started going every day.

His wife was going crazy, and he had to do something before it was too late. Her behavior reminded him of the old days, when she was trying to quit drinking. The experience had taught him that interventions at times like these were difficult and delicate.

He took off his coat and tie, rolled up his sleeves, and entered Serena's observation post.

"So, honey, any news from across the street?"

"I don't like ironic questions."

"I'm not being ironic, I'm just asking you."

"It could have been another question."

"Not when my wife's sitting in the dark staring across the street for hours on end." He turned the light on.

"Who told you I've been here for hours?"

"Nobody needed to; it's obvious you've been here a long time."

"Someone must have said something or you wouldn't know. It's Zuleide. You've been paying the maid to spy on me."

"I am paying her—she's our maid—but not to spy on you."

"You feel really safe, don't you?"

"Not always. Sometimes I feel deeply insecure, especially about you."

"Because you don't trust me."

"I don't mistrust you. I just don't know you, which is something else."

"That's not how you acted about the policeman. The way you were talking, it sounded like I'd had sex with him in the middle of the Avenida Atlântica."

"I just thought it was odd that he would leave work in the middle of the day to come chat and have a juice on the beach with my wife."

"Jesus, Guilherme, I witnessed a murder!"

"You saw a death, probably a suicide, and all the rest is just a possibility."

"So why did the officer listen to me?"

"Because you said you saw a murder. Or something like that. Of course he had to see if your recollection was credible."

"And it seems that he thought it was."

"Everything depends on what you told him. And how."

"What are you insinuating?"

"I'm not insinuating anything, but you can be persuasive when you set your mind to it."

"One more time: what are you insinuating?"

"Damn it, Serena, I'm speaking very clearly, I'm not hinting at anything. I am saying that you can be very imaginative and very persuasive."

"You think I've gone crazy."

"No, but you're talking about this quite a lot."

"Of course I am! Jesus, neither you nor Espinosa believe me."

"Who's Espinosa?"

"The policeman!"

"I didn't know you two were so close."

"What does that mean?"

"I don't know; you're the only one who can answer that."

"No matter what I say, neither of you believe me."

"What don't we believe?"

Serena got up from the chair. The expression in her eyes had changed, and her mouth, usually so lovely and sensual, was pursed.

"You think I'm a useless and deluded woman."

"The policeman said that?"

"No, but that's what he thinks."

"Why do you think that?"

"Jesus, what the fuck, are you going to interrogate me too?"

Serena turned out the light, left her dressing room, went

into the bedroom, came back out, and went to the living room. The table was set, and the maid was ready to serve dinner. Guilherme waited for his wife to decide where she wanted to sit. He sat beside her, close enough to be able to reach out and touch her hand. Serena jerked back her arm as if shocked.

"What's gong on?" he asked.

"What's going on is that I feel like I'm going crazy."

"Why do you say that?"

"Because I don't even know what to believe anymore. From you two asking me so many questions I really don't know what actually happened."

"Sweetheart, whatever happened has nothing to do with you. You didn't cause anyone's death; you didn't even know the person who died. You're not responsible for anything that went on in that apartment."

"For what went on in that apartment, no—"

"So why—"

"—but the officer said that thanks to my story they've changed the direction of the investigation and are looking for whoever might be responsible for the woman's death."

"Fine, let them look. What's the problem?"

"The problem is that I don't know what to think anymore."

"You don't know what to think about what?"

"All I'm sure of is the horror of that woman falling onto the sidewalk."

"Didn't you say you saw her fighting with someone?"

"When I opened the window, I saw the woman in the living room across the street; she was pacing back and forth, talking, and she couldn't have been talking to herself."

"And the purse?"

"A long time ago, I heard a story about a woman who, before she threw herself off a building, threw her purse first. I've remembered that for years. When the woman here fell, I thought I saw a purse falling first. Now I'm not sure if what I saw fall was the purse or the woman."

"Did you tell the officer that?"

"What? The story I heard? I don't even know if it was true."

"So . . ."

"So . . . I don't know anymore. . . . I'm so confused. . . . I don't know if the things I remember happening really happened."

"I'm sorry, dear, but we need to tell the officer that."

"Tell him what? That I'm confused? You think he's not confused? The only one who's not confused is you."

"You . . ."

"You don't need to say anything. I'll take care of the officer. It's my business."

7

He didn't turn on the lights or take off his jacket. He sat down in the rocking chair and stayed there in the dark. He heard sounds that were perfectly distinct from the noise of the street; sometimes he heard a kind of death rattle followed by a profound silence: the refrigerator. He sat so long that his legs went to sleep. It was after midnight when he looked at his watch. He must have been sitting there for almost three hours.

Why would someone wear a cap at night? It was just a fashion. A lot of people did that. It could also be a disguise. And what do you hide with a cap? Baldness: bald people are easy to recognize. If you wanted to hide baldness, though, it would be better to wear a wig. So if someone is wearing a cap at night, it's because they like the look. Serena also said that the killer was wearing a jacket. A cap and jacket: lots of younger people dressed like that. He could imagine the killer in tennis shoes, jeans, a jacket, and a cap, like hundreds of other people walking down the street at any given moment. The jacket worked with the look, but in the heat it was an odd choice. Serena herself had said she was in her dressing room picking out a low-cut dress because it was so hot out. So it was a hot night. Why would someone wear a hat and a jacket, things used to keep warm, on such a hot night? It couldn't be just for the look. The disguise hypothesis worked better. What do you hide with a jacket and a hat?

Over the next four days, which included Saturday and Sunday, Espinosa visited the widows of the murdered policemen. Sunday afternoon also included an unofficial and unauthorized visit to Celeste's apartment. She'd hurried out of the apartment both times, as if fleeing; and people in a hurry always leave something important behind.

Which she had.

The two other days were also dedicated to inquiries at telephone and insurance companies.

8

The new elements he'd obtained from the phone and insurance companies led Espinosa's mind in a direction he hesitated to pursue, but that mounting evidence made it impossible to ignore. The confirmation depended on his having one more chat with Serena, which he could do that evening, as soon as he got out of the shower. He was still drying off when the telephone rang.

"Officer Espinosa?"

"Yes?"

"Detective Everaldo, from the station. Sorry to call at this hour, sir."

"What happened?"

"Another death. I thought I should tell you because it's just like the one in Leme."

"How do you mean?"

"Another girl threw herself off the building."

"Who told you? What building?"

"The sergeant on patrol who went to the scene. It seems like it's the same building."

"Did he get the woman's name?"

"Yes, sir. Serena Rodes."

One of Espinosa's hands gripped the phone, while the other was still rubbing his hair with the towel.

"Call Ramiro, Welber, and Artur. Tell them to meet me at the scene."

On his way to Leme, he tried to gather his wits. It could have been a mistake. Just as they'd confused Rosita with Celeste, they could have mixed up Serena with someone else. He was on the scene in ten minutes. The area had been cordoned off. Two patrol cars and an ambulance from the fire department were parked in front of the building.

It was Serena. The body was less than six feet from where Rosita had landed.

Espinosa spoke to the policemen and sought out the doorman.

"It was before nine, sir. Just like the other one."

"Was she by herself in the apartment?"

"I think she was, sir, but I can't guarantee it. All I can say is that I didn't see anyone go up to the tenth floor."

"Did she cry out?"

"No, sir."

"Is anyone in the apartment?"

"There's a guard at the door."

Espinosa went back to talk to the policemen outside. The only thing they'd managed to learn was that the dead woman's name was Serena Rodes and that she lived across the street.

Two deaths, exactly the same. Except this time Serena wasn't on the other side of the street watching.

Welber and Artur got there at almost exactly the same time.

"Let's go up," he said to them.

The cop guarding the door said that the door was unlocked and that nobody had entered since he'd arrived.

"Before you got here, did anyone go in?"

"I don't know, Chief."

The apartment had not been disturbed. Only one lamp was on. On the living room table sat the packaging of a whiskey bottle: the thin paper that surrounds the bottle and the pieces of plastic that protect it from breaking. The empty bottle lay on the sofa. A little bit of liquid had dripped onto a pillow. No cups in sight.

"I don't think she could have drunk so much whiskey straight out of the bottle," said Espinosa, "unless she was forced to."

"You think someone made her drink?"

"Nothing about Serena suggested that she would get drunk or kill herself. At least, nothing recent."

Espinosa examined the wall and the floor next to the windowsill. There were no lights on in Serena's apartment across the street.

"Sir, there are two cups on the drying rack, along with a teacup, a saucer, and a dessert plate. All dry."

"Why would a person alone need two cups?" asked Artur.

"Because they're lazy," Espinosa answered, thinking of himself. "Or because they were used for two different drinks. Which wouldn't explain why the cups were washed. Or she could have been drinking with someone else. But nobody does the dishes before throwing themselves out of a window."

"They could have been washed by someone else," Artur said.

"I asked them to call in Freire. Try to find out if he's on his way. Try to find her maid. Talk to the doorman across the street."

Ramiro arrived as the boss was trying to track down Guilherme Rodes.

While he was waiting for the forensic examiner to arrive, Espinosa talked with the on-duty registrar at the Forensic Institute, explaining that the dead woman was married to an important member of the federal government: that would light a fire under them. He wanted an autopsy that very night.

Freire arrived in party clothes.

"Did we take you away from some event?"

"A birthday."

"Yours?"

"My father-in-law's."

Espinosa filled him in.

"I saw the body before I came up here. I got her fingerprints," Freire said, displaying two strips of adhesive tape.

The next hour was consumed by forensic matters. Espinosa went down to be present when the body was removed and to notify the Forensic Institute that he would be heading down to supervise the autopsy. Welber and Artur had turned up Serena's maid, who was in a state of shock and couldn't speak rationally. But she did manage to give them a piece of paper with her boss's number in

Brasília. When Freire finished up, Espinosa was getting off the phone with Guilherme Rodes.

"No prints on the cups," Freire said. "On the bottle, I only found hers."

"The bottle was unwrapped right here," Espinosa answered. "If she was alone, we wouldn't find any other prints."

"I thought they were a little farther apart than normal."

"Farther apart?"

"As if someone had pressed her fingers to the bottle, like when you're taking someone's prints. It can happen. What I thought was interesting was that there aren't many prints. A person who drinks a whole bottle of whiskey picks it up several times, leaving lots of prints. I only found two thumbprints and two each of her index, middle, and ring fingers. None of her pinkies, which would be hard to avoid if you're picking up a full bottle. I'll check out the rest of the material and talk to you tomorrow."

Before leaving for the Forensic Institute, Espinosa summoned Ramiro, Welber, and Artur.

"Find Celeste as quickly as possible. I want all three of you to work on this full-time."

The autopsy was to be carried out by the researcher on duty, with whom Espinosa spoke for a few minutes before he began his work. They'd known each other for a few years, so they dispensed with formalities.

"Evening, Doctor. Can I sit with you?"

"Sure. Who's the woman?"

"The wife of a big shot in the federal government."

"What happened? Someone mentioned suicide."

"I think her death is suspicious."

"Let's see what we find."

The body had just arrived and had been placed directly on the autopsy table. The doctor put on his apron and gloves before removing the sheet covering the dead woman. Upon seeing the dead, wounded body, Espinosa closed his eyes and sat remembering Serena dropping her dress to the ground, alive and beautiful in her nudity. He opened his eyes and focused on the examination. Before using the surgical instruments, the doctor performed a meticulous visual examination of the body, paying special attention to her nails and searching for any possible wounds that would have predated the fall.

Less than an hour later, Espinosa left without having shed his suspicions. Besides the fact that Serena had ingested a large quantity of alcohol, Espinosa had also learned that she hadn't had dinner. The doctor had no way of knowing if she had been forced to drink the whiskey or if she had done so voluntarily. He had discovered that she'd been alive when she'd fallen. Probably drunk.

"Do you think someone who was that drunk could climb up onto a windowsill and jump?"

"I think so. It depends on the person's resistance to alcohol. Drunkenness can also produce nausea, and she may have leaned out the window to vomit."

"The windowsill is a little lower than normal," Espinosa added.

"She might have gotten dizzy and lost her balance. She might have even fainted as she was leaning out . . . if you don't buy the idea that she killed herself."

"Thanks, Doctor."

The Rua Mem de Sá was deserted. He could see the Lapa Aqueduct in the distance. Espinosa stood for a while in front of his car, trying to reconcile his two Serenas: the one he'd known alive and the one he'd just seen lying cold on the autopsy table.

9

Two days later, arriving home in the evening, Espinosa found a postcard. An aerial shot of Rio, postmarked from the airport. The message confirmed the conclusion he'd reached over the last few days.

Espinosa dear,

I'd love for you to be here with me. Too bad we're not on the same side. Don't worry about protecting me anymore . . . or trying to find me.

Love,
Celeste

10

The four o'clock shuttle to São Paulo was only two-thirds full, which gave the passengers a little more room. Espinosa preferred the aisle; he didn't like to be scrunched up next to the window, and he didn't think there was much to see at thirty thousand feet. Irene had seemed genuinely surprised when he'd woken her with a call inviting her to dinner that night.

"Is it anything serious?"

"Nothing you need to worry about."

"Honey, you call me from Rio de Janeiro at this hour inviting me to dinner tonight in São Paulo: that's something to worry about."

"But really, there's no need. I just want to be with you. . . . I want to see what you think about a few of my ideas."

"Are these ideas about the girl I gave the dresses to?"

"They are."

"I know a nice quiet place where we can start the conversation. I'll wait for you at the hotel."

At the station, Espinosa had said he needed to go to São Paulo to check out some leads he'd gotten from the insurance companies and the car dealerships. Nobody had thought it was particularly strange, because the chief had been acting strangely for the last few days. Now, with his seat pushed back and his eyes closed, he thought about Irene.

The trip from the airport to the hotel, in a taxi, took twice as long as the plane ride; the traffic was a sure sign he was in São Paulo. At the hotel desk, there was a note from Irene telling him that she'd be back before six-thirty.

At six-thirty, she entered the lobby looking as if she'd spent the whole afternoon getting ready.

"It's still early for dinner," he said. "Why don't we take our things up to the room and kill some time?"

"Instead of killing time, I have another idea."

"That's what I was thinking. What do you want to do: talk, eat, and make love, or the other way around?"

"Hmm . . ."

"We could also make love, talk, eat, and then make love again. That way we cover all our bases."

"That's more like it."

The first step lasted more than two hours, so they decided to combine the second and third steps. They'd have the rest of the night for the fourth.

The restaurant Irene selected was nice, not as noisy as other trendy places, and it was only a few blocks from the hotel. They walked holding hands, like lovers. Which, of course, they were.

She brought it up first.

"What's eating you?"

"The possibility of committing an enormous injustice,

on the one hand . . . and on the other, the possibility of letting someone get away with murder."

"Tell me about it."

They still hadn't ordered. They were drinking wine and
nibbling on the Italian bread.

"What I'm going to tell you can't be said officially.
You're the only person I feel comfortable burdening with
my imaginary extravagances."

Irene sat silently, concentrating on what he was saying.
The whole restaurant seemed to quiet down, lending Espinosa's speech the resonance of the confessional.

"I think I already know the name of the murderer. The
whole time it was so close that we didn't even see it. But a
few days ago, a detail reported by a witness began to take
shape and become more important, so important that I
went into the apartment of one of the people implicated
without a warrant. With what I found there, and what I
managed to learn from the phone and insurance companies, my doubts became certainties. Yesterday, I received a
postcard that seemed to confirm the certainty. From the
very beginning, we had it in our heads that the murderer
was someone from outside, a hired professional unknown
in Rio de Janeiro. We looked for months for someone intelligent enough to pull off the murders. It never occurred to
anyone that it might not be a man."

"And it was a woman?"

"Nobody thought of that, not even the victims, which is
why they were killed so easily. They were all killed by
someone who could get close to them without raising any

suspicions, someone they trusted, both the cops and the women, someone who knew their habits, who could ring the bell or knock on the door and be welcomed by the un-armed victim. Someone who even in the middle of the street would attract no attention, from the victim or the lo-cals. . . . A woman. Someone smart and competent. A woman like Celeste."

"The woman I lent the clothes to?"

"The same."

"And what about the attacks on her? Wasn't she the one you were hiding and protecting?"

"She was never in any danger. Nobody ever busted into her apartment, except me and my staff. Nobody tried to kill her. That's what she told us, but we didn't check it out. I was protecting her from us."

"And the killer you've been talking about?"

"He never existed."

"But . . ."

"Nothing's definitive; lots of things still have to be cleared up, lots of holes still have to be filled in—and not just by my imagination. For now this story is pure fiction. I hope someday, once and for all, we'll get to the truth. Here goes: Ramos, Silveira, and Nestor, the three cops who were killed, weren't brilliant people. They were completely mediocre, so much so that nobody ever noticed them. And they weren't honest, either. They had worked together be-fore, in the robbery division, and realized that there was money to be made from stolen cars. Celeste was Nestor's mistress, and she sat in on the group's meetings. She quickly realized that there was a lot more money in the detectives' scam than they realized. She was smarter and better educated, and she spoke some Spanish and English, which made it easier to work with foreigners. She came up with a much more sophisticated plan and suggested that they test-drive it for a few months. If they were happy with the results, all they'd have to do was carry on. They accepted. There was nothing to lose. The plan was a big success, and they decided to stick with it. From what I gathered from the insurance companies and secondhand-auto-parts dealers, the plan included getting middle-class kids to steal cars and then have the police "recover" them—the police being the three of them. Then they would cut a deal with the insurance companies and the cars' owners. They also stole imported cars for resale in provincial cities and Paraguay; and they stole luxury cars, foreign and domestic, for parts. The whole thing depended on the support of cops from several places. Celeste reorganized the bribery system already in place, paying out even better tips. The enterprise moved full speed ahead, well oiled and completely secure. The base of operations was a garage in the Zona Oeste. They made a lot of money. Much more than they'd imagined. And the business was extremely safe. It didn't depend on murder or violence against third parties. There was an important detail: Celeste decided that only a very small portion of the proceeds could be used for buying material goods, so as not to draw attention to themselves. Most of the money was exchanged for dollars and secreted abroad. They agreed not to touch the money for a few years, at which point the money would be divided up. I think that Celeste decided to keep all the money right before she was going to have to divvy it up. She drew up a list of everyone on the take, which included both precinct chiefs and detectives as well as local politicians, and deposited copies of the list, in addressed envelopes, in a safe-deposit box. She hired a lawyer and gave him a letter instructing him to send the lists to several people in case she was killed."

"And what did she do to get her hands on the money?"

"The only thing she could."

"She killed the others?"

"That's what I think."

"Shot them?"

"It's clean. Silent, no physical contact."

"And her friend? She wasn't thrown out the window?"

"We thought the killer had made a mistake. Not knowing Celeste and going only on a description—a description that fit both of them—he killed the wrong woman. But that was when we thought we were dealing with a hired gun. Now I think that Celeste herself pushed Rosita out of the window. Which made her seem like the next victim. A perfect alibi."

"Espinosa, how does a woman my size mange to push another one out of a window?"

"By throwing her purse out first."

"What?"

"They were fighting in the living room—according to a witness. For some reason, Celeste throws her friend's purse out of the window. When the friend, shocked, runs over to see where her purse fell, Celeste comes up from behind; the friend is dangling over the windowsill, and . . ."

"That's evil!"

"I don't think it was planned. What was evil was knowing exactly how to take advantage of the situation."

"A few days ago you thought she'd be the next victim. What made you change your mind?"

"The cap."

"The cap?"

"The cap I found in her apartment."

"What does that prove?"

"A witness who saw the fight, who lived across the street and saw the purse fly out of the window, said that the person fighting with Rosita was wearing a cap and a jacket. Why would someone wear a cap and a jacket on a hot summer day? It could only be as a disguise. Celeste is as tall as a man of medium height. I found a cap and three different jackets in her wardrobe. Besides, I remembered that one of the people we interviewed about the first murder said that the male nurse who went up in the elevator with the old man in the wheelchair was wearing a cap—"

"So what? I have plenty of jackets and more than one cap."

"But you never sent me a postcard from the airport on your way out of the country, telling me it's too bad we weren't on the same side."

"You mean that she not only borrowed my clothes but my boyfriend as well?"

"Just your clothes. Your boyfriend was indeed used, but not in the way you think."

"I know. You're not going to get her?"

"Under what charge?"

"Murder. Didn't she kill six people?"

"Maybe even seven. The witness who lived across the street died in circumstances that will probably never entirely be explained. But listen, this is just a story. Most of it is based on suppositions; a little bit can be deduced, but I don't have any proof. There's still a lot I've just dreamed up—maybe even most of it."

"And so?"

"So for now it's just a story."

"You're not going to do anything?"

"By now she must be miles away, in some foreign country. I'd bet on some Caribbean tax haven. The whole time she said she was hiding from the murderer she was putting the finishing touches on a plan she'd been developing for a long time."

"She sent the clothes back."

"I thought she would."

"With a note of thanks."

"She's not your average criminal. Crime, for her, is a question of logic, not ethics."

"For me, she's just a faceless size six."

"Her face is quite attractive."

"You were all—including the victims—seduced by her. You think she's going to get off scot-free?"

"I don't think so. She's smart, but she's too self-confident. After a while, she'll feel safe enough to risk coming back to Brazil. By then I'll have all the proof. And I'll be waiting for her."

"It's terrible. Someone with no criminal record murders her boyfriend, two friends, and three girlfriends—six people, or seven, as you said—while making everybody think she's a poor vulnerable girl threatened by a ferocious assassin."

"We still don't know if she has a criminal record. She could be using an assumed name."

"Are you completely sure about what you've told me?"

"In my heart of hearts. That's why I'm talking to you. Being sure doesn't necessarily mean knowing the truth. It's intimate, subjective."

"What do you need to go from certainty to truth?"

"Facts."

"Aren't the murders the facts?"

"The only facts in this whole story."

"What are you going to do?"

"Order dinner."

ABOUT THE AUTHOR

A distinguished academic, Luiz Alfredo Garcia-Roza is a best-selling novelist who lives in Rio de Janeiro. The first book in the Espinosa series, *The Silence of the Rain*, was published in 2002 by Henry Holt to critical acclaim, followed by *December Heat* (2003) and *Southwesterly Wind* (2004).